The
SCHUYLER HOUSE

Cade Haddock Strong

BELLA
BOOKS
2017

Bella Books, Inc.
P.O. Box 10543
Tallahassee, FL 32302

Printed in the United States of America on acid-free paper.

First Bella Books Edition 2017

Editor: Amanda Jean
Cover Designer: Judith Fellows

ISBN: 978-1-59493-572-5

About the Author

Cade Haddock Strong currently lives in Washington, DC. She loves skiing, biking, hiking, running, and playing golf and makes a valiant effort to keep up on current events. She and her wife have lived all over the US and abroad and they love to travel.

Acknowledgments

Thank you to my editor, Amanda Jean, for her awesome suggestions on how to strengthen the storyline of this novel.

Thank you to my parents for giving me a great education that nurtured my love of writing.

Thank you to my amazing friend Mary Moon Marshburn for inspiring the cover design.

Thank you to my wife Lisa, who believed in me and supported me while I wrote this book, who patiently listened as I dreamed up plot ideas and who read countless drafts. Mostly though, thank you for being proud of me. That made all the difference.

Dedication

For my wife Lisa. You are my rock.

CHAPTER ONE

There are four of us. We all grew up in Vermont and, although we each wandered off to other places after high school, we all ended up back in the Green Mountain State for one reason or another. We're all strong, independent women, and we have what you might call a unique "hobby"—we are art thieves. Over the past five years, we've successfully pulled off nearly a dozen burglaries and to my total amazement we've never gotten caught. We plan each heist meticulously but, even so, there have been a few close calls.

Without exception, we sell all the pieces we steal, and we've made a decent amount of money doing it. Of course, we know it's all terribly illegal, not to mention wrong, but the thrill of it is completely addicting.

Currently, we're hovering around Sarah Finnegan's large computer screen. Sarah is our de facto leader. She and I have been friends since grade school, and she's the only person in the entire world allowed to call me by my given name, Matilda. I've always despised the name, and I've gone by Mattie since I was a little kid. Sarah is also the first person I came out to when I realized I was gay my senior year of high school. She's the only one of the four of us who has kids, although she and her husband Jake split up a few years ago and now share custody of their two boys.

Sarah has the floor plans for our next target—the Schuyler House—up on her screen. We're all staring at it intently as she walks us through its various quirks.

"As you guys can see, the layout of the house is a jumbled mess," Sarah says. "It looks like the house was added on to multiple times without consideration for how the pieces fit together."

"Yeah, wait till you see the place. There are all these weird passageways that lead to nowhere, and a couple of the rooms are so tiny that you can barely fit a chair and table in them. It's really bizarre," Kat says.

Kat Conroy is the only one of the four of us with any real art background. She has a master's degree in art history and used to work at a gallery in Washington, DC. She first flagged the Schuyler House as a potential target over a year ago. Its art collection is renowned, and our reconnaissance to date indicated that security was a bit looser than you might find at a typical art museum. Our intel was aided by the fact that Kat scored an invitation to attend an artist's retreat sponsored by the Schuyler House. While Kat was at the retreat, she was able to fully scope out the property, evaluate the floor plan and study the various security procedures they have in place. She also had plenty of time to confirm the exact location of some of the pieces we hoped to acquire.

Up until about twenty years ago, Schuyler House was part of the Schuyler Estate—a massive property in upstate New York. Back in the day, the estate was comprised of the main house, multiple outbuildings, and about one thousand acres of land. Eventually, the estate's upkeep became too much for the remaining heirs. Rather than selling it all off, they sold most of the land but held on to the main house and converted it into a retreat for artists and writers. The retreat quickly became an icon in the contemporary art world, attracting artists from all over the world who came for the enlightening, and often raucous, retreats but also in order to flock beneath the astonishing art collection adorning the walls of the main house.

Schuyler House is extremely secluded. It's located in a very rural part of New York State that most people don't even know exists—the Adirondacks, a state park that also happens to be the largest park in the contiguous United States. It's huge at more than 6.1 million acres, a land area greater than Yellowstone, Yosemite, Grand Canyon, Glacier, and the Great Smoky Mountains National Parks combined. Most people think of Manhattan when they think of New York State, yet the vast majority of the state is actually fairly rural. The Adirondacks are unique too in that something like half of the land within the park is privately, rather than publicly, owned.

The house is located just outside the boundary of the Adirondacks and sits at the end of a three-mile long dirt driveway. The estate itself is nestled at the edge of a forest, and a river runs directly behind the main house. Not surprisingly, that area of New York gets a lot of snow in the winter, much more than other parts of the state due to its proximity to the Great Lakes. As a result, lake-effect snow frequently hits. Lake-effect snow is typically isolated to only a small geographic area, leading to huge regional differences in snowfall. I've seen times where the towns near the lake get hit with twenty inches of snow while a town only ten miles away barely gets a dusting. It's really strange.

The Schuyler family art collection was started by Duncan Schuyler in the early 1900s. He collected art through his entire life, mostly impressionist and modern art by American and European artists—Cézanne, Gauguin, Bonnard, Matisse, O'Keeffe, and Kandinsky, to name a few. Near the end of his life he, and later his wife and daughter, also started to collect famous photographs. Our goal is to steal five lower-tier pieces from the collection.

Just like all our previous heists, we've spent countless hours researching and planning for the Schuyler House burglary.

There's absolutely no reason to think anything will go wrong, but for some reason Sarah has a bad vibe about this burglary.

"I don't know, I just can't shake this weird feeling I have about the Schuyler House," Sarah explains after we're done looking at the floor plan. "The only reason I'm not pulling the plug is because I seriously need the money. I've got like three hundred dollars in my checking account and the boys are headed off to college soon…I've saved almost nothing for their tuition."

I rub her upper back gently. "Do you think we've missed something in our planning?"

"No, nothing like that," she replies.

"What is it then?" Kat asks.

"It's just that the house is so isolated and its floor plan is so tricky. I feel like we're walking into a maze and we're going to get trapped. Plus, we've been so damn lucky, and that luck has got to run out sometime, right?" Sarah asks.

"I hear you, but I'm actually feeling good about this one. The security they've got is the weakest I've ever seen for a collection of this caliber," Kat replies.

"I'm with Kat. This one feels easy compared to some of our other heists. I'm pumped about it," Ellen pipes in.

Ellen Church is the fourth woman in our group. She's nearly six feet tall and is absolutely stunning with long, silky dark-brown hair, dark-brown eyes, and olive skin. Most people think she's Latina, but she's not. She went to Harvard Law School and went on to work for a high-powered law firm in New York. She even made partner but finally hung up her power suits for good when her marriage fell apart. I think she did pretty well in the divorce, but she never really talks about it. She doesn't practice law anymore either. She moved back to Vermont after her divorce and now spends most of her time helping her brother tend to his Christmas tree farm.

"Plus, our plan is totally brilliant!" Ellen adds.

"It is pretty brilliant," Sarah admits.

I have to agree. We've decided to rob the estate in the middle of a massive snowstorm. We came up with idea because a major blizzard hit Schuyler House when Kat was there for the artists retreat and the Schuyler House staff was totally unprepared for the big storm: they only have one snowplow truck and it was not enough to keep up with the unrelenting snow that inundated the long driveway. Kat, along with all the other retreat attendees, was stranded for two extra days. Not that the impassable driveway really mattered that much anyway since most of the flights in and out of the nearby airport were canceled due to the storm.

At any rate, once we learned that the Schuyler House staff struggled to maintain the estate's driveway in the winter, we had an "aha" moment—vehicles, namely police vehicles, would have a tough time getting up the private driveway during a major snowstorm. Certainly, beneficial for would-be burglars. Of course, it also means that it will be extremely difficult, if not impossible, for us to reach the estate by car, but we didn't let that deter us. That area of the state is a snowmobile haven, and it has more miles of snowmobile trails than it does roads. It should be relatively easy to approach the house by snowmobile during a major snowstorm. We're just waiting for the weather forecasters to give us our cue.

CHAPTER TWO

The four of us weren't always art thieves. In fact, most of us have day jobs. I, for instance, am a partner in a small forensic accounting firm in Burlington.

The road to becoming art thieves started more than five years ago. Sarah and I were in New York City for our friend Sandy's wedding, and while we were there, thieves slipped into an Upper East Side row house and made off with two incredibly valuable paintings.

Sarah read about the burglary in the *New York Times* and became completely fixated on the story. She couldn't believe how simple the plot seemed. In the weeks that followed the wedding, Sarah obsessively combed the Internet for recent burglaries from private collections, amazed at how many had taken place in just the last few years, even in this age of supposed high-tech security. Not surprisingly, the burglaries she read about took place all over the world—wherever rich people lived. Further, a pretty low percentage of the stolen pieces were ever recovered and an even lower percentage of the culprits were ever apprehended.

Over the next few months, Sarah decided she could do it—
slip into someone's house and make off with some high-priced
piece of art.

* * *

Sarah confessed her plan to me one summer night when
we were at a beach party and three sheets to the wind. I just
laughed when she told me because we were both drunk and I
didn't think she was even remotely serious.

A few days later, I ran into Sarah on the bike path in
Burlington and she asked if I remembered our conversation at
the beach party. I told her that I thought she was kidding, and
she made it clear that she was dead serious. I still didn't believe
her because she's about the most law-abiding person I know.
She doesn't even drive over the speed limit. I pressed her to
explain this sudden desire to become a criminal, and she told me
she was sick of being boring and that she was having a midlife
crisis a little bit early. She also admitted that money was pretty
tight and a little extra cash wouldn't hurt.

When I was still non-committal, Sarah chided me and
brought up the fact that I've always had a wild side and that
stealing art should be right up my alley. I'm not sure about the
"right up my alley" part, but she was right about me having
a wild side. I may be an accountant, but I've done crazy stuff
my whole life: I stole my parent's car on numerous occasions
well before I was of legal driving age; I hitchhiked to Florida
for spring break when I was in high school; I nearly died on a
back-country ski adventure when I got lost and had to spend the
night in the woods in the dead of winter.

It took a while, but finally Sarah convinced me to join her.
From then on, Sarah and I met regularly to either jog or bike.
While we worked out, we began to build a plan. One of the first
things we did was to establish two fairly basic guidelines to help
direct our future decisions about what to steal and from where.

In terms of what to steal, we decided to focus on lower-tier
pieces from impressive collections. In other words, we wanted

to target pieces of significant value, but not "trophy" or standout pieces like those stolen from the Isabella Stewart Gardner Museum. In terms of where to target, we decided to avoid major museums and instead focus on small private collections.

We aim for lower-tier pieces in impressive collections because it's possible to make decent money stealing the lower tier-pieces but law enforcement is likely to be hesitant to throw major resources into finding them and institutions are less likely to offer large rewards for their return. Some thieves actually target pieces they think they can then turn around and "return" to the museum for a reward, but quickly we decided we'd leave that MO to low-level criminals, especially because a large reward usually inspires more people to expend resources to locate stolen works.

The decision to avoid major museums was a no-brainer since big museums are likely to have more sophisticated security than private collections. Furthermore, many large museums now attach RFID tags or GPS tracking devices to many of their pieces. Not surprisingly, most small private collections just don't have the resources for this kind of technology.

Given that there are literally thousands of places in the United States alone that house incredibly valuable art, we figure these two guidelines would, if nothing else, help us to whittle down the list of targets on which to focus our research and scouting. Of course, we also hope these guidelines would help keep us out of jail, but we try to avoid even thinking about that possibility.

* * *

Sarah and I decided we needed to expand beyond our gang of two and try to recruit someone else to join us.

"What about Kat?" Sarah asked while we were debating who to recruit.

Kat seemed like an obvious choice to me. She's been our friend for eons, and her extensive art background would bring a whole new level of the art expertise to our discussions.

"Think we can convince her to come over to the dark side?" Sarah asked.

I replied that I felt pretty certain that we could. I knew Kat loved art. It would probably pain her to steal it, but after her experience in DC, I knew she was pretty jaded about the art world and might want to get a little revenge.

Kat was fired from her dream job at Siddons Fine Art in DC. She strongly advised a wealthy collector not to purchase a piece he was considering. She warned him that the seller had a shady reputation and that the piece could be a fake. He, of course, blew her off and bought it anyway. It turns out it was a fake and the collector was irate. He told Kat's boss that she'd encouraged him to buy it, probably because he'd been too embarrassed to admit he'd been duped. Of course, the owner of Siddons believed the collector and promptly fired Kat and told her she would never work in the art world again.

We decided to invite Kat to go for a hike so we could lay out our plan.

* * *

A few days later, Sarah and I described our burgeoning plan to Kat as the three of us trudged along the Camel's Hump Trail. I was nervous to see how she would react.

"You guys are fucking crazy," Kat said once we finished describing our plan. "But that's why I love you!"

"So, you want to join us?" Sarah asked. "It could be your chance to get a little revenge after what happened in DC."

Kat admitted that she was intrigued. She hadn't been able to get a decent job since the incident in DC, and she was understandably still extremely angry about the whole thing. She agreed to help us do research but said she needed a little more time before she could decide whether she'd get more involved.

Before long, Kat and Sarah started spending hours together to pore over obscure art blogs, art history journals, and various other scholarly publications. Kat's addition to the group really helped us refine our process for deciding which pieces and places to target.

* * *

Ellen became our fourth and final member. Ellen is a few years older than me, and even though we both grew up in the same town, we didn't actually meet until we both attended Sandy's wedding in New York.

When Ellen moved back to Vermont after her divorce, she happened to join a women's cycling group Sarah was in. During one of Ellen's first rides with the group, she and Sarah realized that they'd actually met before: they both knew Sandy and attended her wedding in New York. Anyway, Ellen and Sarah became fast friends.

Ellen, Kat, Sarah, and I all started spending a lot of time together. Ellen is so carefree and funny, and it was hard for me to imagine her as a buttoned-up lawyer. I quickly discovered she's even crazier than me. She has a motorcycle she drives like a bat out of hell, and she goes skydiving every chance she gets. It's like she lived the early part of her life doing what everyone expected of her and now she's living life on her terms. The first time she got wind of our plot to steal art, she thought it was a joke. When she realized we were completely serious, she wanted in on the action. Like me, she was addicted to the thrill from day one.

CHAPTER THREE

Once we were a gang of four, we started to devise a plan for our first heist in earnest. It quickly became obvious to all of us that stealing the art would be the easy part; turning the stolen art into cash would be significantly more difficult. It's not like we could walk into some gallery or auction house and try to sell a famous piece of stolen art.

It was during these initial conversations that I remembered a boy named Olivier. Olivier is French, and I met him in high school while I was visiting my aunt and uncle on their small farm about two hours northwest of Paris. My aunt is French, and she and my uncle met when she was an exchange student in the US. They eventually married and decided to settle in France, and I spent nearly every summer with them until I went to college. Olivier and his family lived on the farm that bordered my aunt and uncle's property, and he and I spent countless hours together exploring the countryside. As luck would have it, Olivier's grandfather was a shady art dealer in the outskirts of Paris and Olivier went to work for him after high school.

Olivier eventually became our fencer. I have no idea what he does with the pieces after we hand them over to him. I am not sure any of us ever wanted to know. Maybe they smuggle them into Russia or China or maybe they are involved with the mob or something.

We consult Olivier when we're in the early stages of planning a heist, just to make sure he's interested in the pieces we're considering and to discuss a ballpark figure he would be willing to pay for them. All our communication with Olivier takes place on a super secure channel he set up so that none of it can ever be traced, and we often exchange dozens of messages with him before and after a heist. Every aspect of the "drop"— the actual way in which we deliver the art to his associates—is very carefully scripted, and he always follows the same exact procedure to get us our payment.

Once we carry out a heist, the four of us are always eager to pass the stolen art on to Olivier as quickly as possible. We don't want to get caught red-handed, and we don't want to worry about transporting the art long distances. Generally, we notify Olivier as soon as we actually have the stolen pieces in our possession—usually within forty-eight hours of the heist— and he responds with the name of a city somewhere within a few hundred miles of the location where we carried out the heist. I honestly have no idea how or why he picks the city for the actual drop, but presumably he picks a place where he has a trusted associate somewhere nearby.

After he gives us the name of the city, it's up to the four of us to pick a physical location in or near the designated city to which we will deliver the art. We contact Olivier again after we've left the art somewhere for him and let him know where to find it. We do it this way so we never have to meet his associates in person and his associate (and any law enforcement or shady characters with whom the associate is involved) never knows where the art was dropped until after we've vacated the premises. Payment usually takes place a few weeks later once Olivier and/ or his associates have the art in their possession and they've had time to examine the pieces. Our payment is always delivered to the same place: Colonial Storage, a giant self-storage facility in the suburbs of Boston.

Olivier pays us in US dollars about seventy-five percent of the time and in euro about twenty-five percent of the time. I used to protest whenever he paid us in euros rather than dollars until I read an article in *The Economist* about an effort by some international law enforcement agencies to eliminate high-denomination notes from various currencies (i.e. the hundred-dollar bill in the US and the S$10,000 note in Singapore). Apparently, law enforcement is making this push because, they argue, high-denomination notes are rarely used for legitimate purposes and are instead primarily used by criminals. Criminals, of course, are most likely to operate in a cash-only world and high-denomination notes are convenient because they're easier to transport. It's much easier to stuff fifty $100 bills in your pocket than five hundred $10 bills, for example. What interested me most about the article was that it included a graphic depicting the weight of ten million dollars (or its equivalent) in cash if paid using various currencies. According to the graphic, ten million in cash weighs a lot more if it's in dollars (about two hundred twenty pounds) than the equivalent amount does in euros (about forty-six pounds) because the highest denomination in the US is the one hundred dollar bill whereas Europe has a €500 note.

Over the past five years, Olivier has paid us millions of dollars for the art we've stolen and sold to him. It amazes me how much money we've made even given the fact that we sell Olivier the art for a fraction of what it would fetch in the legit art world.

From the very beginning, the four of us decided to set aside approximately ten percent of the cash we make and deposit it into what we refer to as our "operating account"—an actual checking account that we opened under the name of Hatshepsut Consulting, a limited liability company we set up. Hatshepsut was a female pharaoh during the Eighteenth Dynasty of Ancient Egypt, so we thought that would be a cool name for our shell company. We established the checking account primarily so that we'd have a joint account from which we could cover costs for stuff like reconnaissance expenses (hotels, travel, and supplies during our scouting missions) and all the supplies we have to buy to actually carry out the burglaries. However, we also opened the checking account to establish an emergency fund—a fund we can access if something goes terribly wrong with a burglary and we need to get our hands on a large amount of untraceable cash quickly.

When we opened the bank accounts, we also rented a safe deposit box at a bank in New York City and registered it to Hatshepsut Consulting. So far, we've managed to set aside more than one million dollars—about half is in the Hatshepsut checking account and the other half we keep in cash in the safe deposit box in New York.

After we set aside money for our expenses and emergency fund, we divide the remaining ninety percent of the proceeds evenly between the four of us. I give away a lot of my money to various charities—not that being all Robin Hood excuses what we do but it somehow makes me feel a heck of a lot better about it—and I pretty much squirrel away the rest. I guess I'm saving it for a rainy day.

The only one of us that has really blown through all of her proceeds is Sarah, and that's mostly because of her ex-husband. Before they were divorced, Jake took most of the money she brought home and pumped it into "sure thing" investments and cockamamie business ideas. When he'd blow through the proceeds from one burglary, he'd start pushing Sarah to pull off another heist. By the time they got divorced, the two of them were actually in some pretty deep debt. Sarah's only recently gotten herself in the black and just started to put away a little money in a college fund for her boys.

CHAPTER FOUR

We didn't have to wait long for the weatherman's cue. The forecasters started calling for another massive storm to hit the area around Schuyler House only a few weeks after Kat returned from the artists' retreat. As luck would have it, a blizzard is supposed to hit on Christmas Eve.

The four of us reconvene at Sarah's house right after news of the storm appears so we can make all of our final preparations for the burglary.

"We totally hit the jackpot!" Ellen declares as soon as the four of us are gathered together. "I mean a major snowstorm on a major holiday. That means security details will likely be sparse and local police resources are likely to be severely strained."

"Yeah, a serious jackpot," Kat reiterates. "It doesn't take a rocket scientist to figure out there was a reason thieves targeted the Isabelle Stewart Gardner Museum in the wee hours of St. Patrick's Day in the heavily Irish City of Boston—the cops were most certainly overwhelmed herding drunks."

"You still got cold feet, Sarah?" I ask.

"They are warming up a little bit," she replies and feigns a smile.

"Come on Sar, the burglary gods are shining on us," Ellen says encouragingly.

"I know. Still, I think this one may be it for me," Sarah replies.

"But you are our fearless leader!" Kat says in protest.

"Ha ha. Well, we'll see. Check back with me and see how I feel after we pull this one off," Sarah says.

"The boys with Jake for Christmas Eve?" I ask in an effort to change the subject. Somehow, the conversation is making me a little uneasy.

"Yeah, they're with him tonight, but I'm supposed to pick them up around noon tomorrow once we're back."

"Does Jake know we're planning another hit?" Ellen asks.

"No, I figured there was no reason to tell him. Things are generally cordial between us, but I still don't trust him," Sarah replies.

"Seems wise," I reply. I've never really liked Jake. He's friendly enough, but there's something shady about him.

"Well, we should probably get to work, huh?" Sarah asks. "We've got less than seventy-two hours until showtime."

We start by confirming the pieces we plan to grab and reviewing their exact location in the house, and then we go over the basic plan of attack for like the thousandth time. After that, we inventory our supplies and make a list of the things we still need to buy.

I'm encouraged that Sarah's mood appears to improve dramatically as we work through the logistics. She's always loved the planning component of the burglaries more than actually carrying them out. Ellen and I, on the other hand, thrive on the thrill of the burglaries themselves. I think Kat loves the planning as much as Sarah and the action as much as me and Ellen.

CHAPTER FIVE

Sarah's house is a flurry of activity the morning of December 24th as we get ready to take off toward Schuyler House. My job is to keep an eye on the weather, and I monitor it obsessively while the others load up all the supplies we need for the heist. All of the weathermen and women are predicting a very, *very* white Christmas. In fact, upstate New York is expected to get its largest snowstorm since meteorologists started keeping track way back in the early 1900s. All the news channels are discussing the impending storm ad nauseam, plastering the TV with photos of scary-looking radar images and completely empty grocery store shelves. The snow hasn't started yet, but if the weathermen are right, it should start coming down any minute.

Eventually, I decide to take a break from watching the weather and head outside to see how the others are doing with the preparations.

The snow crunches under my boots as I walk toward Ellen and Kat as they try to attach a snowmobile trailer to the back of Ellen's black Chevy Tahoe. "Hey guys, you need a hand?" I ask.

"Sure," Ellen replies. "We are having a tough time getting the hitch pin in place." She points vaguely to the back of the Tahoe.

"A what pin?" I ask.

Ellen rolls her eyes at my obvious lack of trailer-hitch knowledge. "The little pin that locks the trailer to the hitch on the back of the Tahoe," she explains in a know-it-all voice.

I give her a friendly punch to the arm. "Smart-ass!"

It takes some work, but we finally get the pin the way Ellen says it should be and set up the electric connection so the trailer will have taillights. Once the trailer is properly attached to the SUV, we turn our energy to loading our two recently purchased snowmobiles up on to the trailer.

Even though we all live in Vermont, none of us are big into snowmobiling, and as a result, none of us actually owned a snowmobile when we came up with the idea to rob Schuyler House during a snowstorm. Snowmobiles are not cheap, and we considered renting them but ultimately concluded that renting would be too risky. The stores that rent them require all sorts of credit card deposits and most want to see ID. So, we decided to purchase two snowmobiles of our own. We combed Craigslist for a decent set of used snowmobiles and settled on a pair some guy was selling in New Hampshire. The snowmobiles are only a few years old, and the fact that the seller is in New Hampshire was an added bonus because New Hampshire is significantly more lax about registering the snow machines than the State of Vermont.

In addition to the snowmobiles, we also bought two steel utility sleds we found on eBay. These metal utility sleds look like mini sleighs and are designed to attach to the back of a snowmobile so you can drag stuff along behind you while you ride. We plan to use them to drag the art from the Schuyler House back to the SUV.

At any rate, after we get the snowmobiles loaded up on the trailer, I head into Sarah's garage to find the steel utility sleds, and we strap those onto the trailer alongside the snowmobiles.

Next, we load our supplies into the back of the SUV. We have bottled water, four snowmobile helmets, flashlights, a canvas pouch with a hammer, screwdriver, and a small crowbar, bungee cords, some rope, two heavy-duty black plastic sleds, and a handful of vinyl covers. I picked up the black plastic sleds at Home Depot; they were advertising them as sleds for hauling heavy objects like firewood in the snow, and we plan to use them to drag the art the short distance from the house back to the snowmobiles. We have rough dimensions for all the pieces that we plan to steal so I ordered custom vinyl covers from a place called The Cover Store that I found online. The covers aren't the best quality, but they'll do the trick. I ordered them in early December and luckily, they arrived on time—we weren't expecting another big snowstorm this early in the season.

Each of us has also packed a small duffel with winter attire such as hats, gloves, goggles, fleece pants, ski coats, and snow pants. The duffels get loaded in the SUV too, and the four of us finally climb into the Tahoe and hit the road just after four o'clock in the afternoon. The plan is to drive the SUV to within about ten miles of Schuyler House and leave the SUV at the trailhead for a snowmobile trail that runs right through the property.

The days are really short this time of year so the sun is about to set and the snow has been coming down pretty heavily for the last few hours. In good weather, the drive would take us almost four hours, but given the weather and road conditions, it could take us more like five or six to reach the trailhead where we plan to leave the SUV. As we get close to Schuyler House, every other vehicle on the road seems to be pulling snowmobiles. In this neck of the woods a SUV trailering two snowmobiles blends in like a cow at the state fair.

It is almost ten o'clock at night by the time we finally pull off Route 29A and onto Chicken Foot Road, the road on which the trailhead is located. Chicken Foot Road hasn't been plowed in a few hours, and even in four-wheel drive, the Tahoe struggles somewhat to get through the deep snow. Luckily, the trailhead is only about a quarter mile up Chicken Foot Road, and Ellen expertly navigates the SUV into the small parking lot next to the trailhead. Given that it is Christmas Eve, there are no other cars parked.

Ellen leaves the car running, and we all change into our winter clothes and double-check our supplies before we head out into the snow to unload the snowmobiles. Once we get the snowmobiles down, Ellen and I attach one utility sled to the back of each snowmobile while Kat and Sarah secure our supplies with bungee cords and rope. Finally, it's showtime and I feel my nerves acting up—I love the thrill of pulling off the heists, but I would be lying if I said I didn't get a wee bit nervous. I try to pull my helmet over my ponytail but it's too snug, so I reluctantly pull out my ponytail and let my long blond hair fall over my shoulders. Once we've donned our helmets, we do a quick round of fist bumps and turn toward the snowmobiles.

Ellen climbs on the first snowmobile and Kat slips behind her. Sarah and I both eye the second snowmobile. "You and Ellen practiced driving these things, right?" Sarah asks while she fidgets with the strap of her helmet.

"Yeah, it's a total piece of cake," I say with a confident chuckle as I climb onto the driver's seat. Sarah reluctantly climbs on behind me after I fire up my machine, and I look over at Ellen and give her thumbs-up to indicate we're ready to go. Ellen squeezes the throttle on her snowmobile, and slowly Sarah and I follow her and Kat out of the small parking lot and onto the trail.

I have to admit it's sort of fun to drive the snowmobiles through so much fresh snow. Even with the roar of the snowmobile engines, it feels almost peaceful—we're pretty much in the middle of nowhere and the trail through the woods is pitch black minus the beams of light emitting from our headlights. The trail cuts through a heavily wooded area, and our headlights bounce off the snow-covered trees that line the trail.

It takes us about thirty minutes to reach the Schuyler House. As we approach the estate, we slow down and park our rides off to the side of the snowmobile trail at the point where it comes closest to the main house. We grab our supplies and set off on foot toward the main house. The snow is incredibly deep, and I curse myself for not thinking to bring snowshoes as we trudge through drifts that are thigh deep. It takes us nearly ten minutes to travel the three hundred yards to the house from where we parked.

The main house is built into the side of a hill, and the back deck hangs over a large cliff that leads down to a fast-moving river. We head for the west side of the house where there's a side entrance as well as a set of wooden steps that lead up to a large deck. Once we reach the steps to the deck, we stick the black plastic Home Depot sleds in a snowbank and head up the stairs. We plan to gain access to the house by climbing through one of the windows that overlook the deck because, as Kat discovered while attending the retreat, the doors off the deck are wired for the burglar alarm but the windows are not.

Once we have the art, we plan to exit the house using the side entrance near where we left the Home Depot sleds. If the guard on duty activated the alarm then we will most certainly set it off when we open the side door to escape, but this is a risk we are willing to take. Two of the pieces we plan to steal are fairly large, and it will be much easier to take them out the side entrance rather than try to maneuver them back down the steps from the deck. We're banking on the fact that, given the snow, it will take the police at least thirty minutes to reach the house via the long dirt driveway, and possibly even longer than that. This will leave us more than enough time to drag the art back to the snowmobiles and disappear into the forest. Kat confirmed that the guards at the Schuyler House are unarmed—fortunately, we don't have to worry about being shot at while we escape.

The steps leading up to the deck are treacherous, and we have to kick our boots into the snow as we work our way up them. I'm breathing hard by the time we finally get up the thirty steps to the deck only to find that, unsurprisingly, it hasn't been shoveled recently either and is covered in at least two feet of snow. The deck is dimly lit, illuminated only by small lamps that hang over each door.

We work our way across the deck until we reach one of the windows and pause to stand before it.

"Well, here goes nothing," Ellen says as she digs a hammer and small crowbar out of her backpack so she can jimmy open the window.

We all watch her in silence, and in less than a minute she has the window open. Ellen stuffs the tools back in her coat, gives us all a nod, slowly slips inside without incident and disappears into the darkness of the house. We all wait on the deck while she completes her first task: check on the guard's location and peek in the guardroom. The guardroom is a small room up near the front of the house that has a few computer screens displaying images from the security cameras around the property, but not from the back deck since no security camera is installed there.

Ellen returns less than three minutes later. "Good news! It looks like there is only one guard on duty tonight and he's lying on a couch outside the security booth watching a movie on his iPad," she whispers. "Apparently, the Schuyler House had to settle for the B-team security on Christmas Eve. Lucky for us!" Kat murmurs with a smile.

Sarah nods. "Well, no time like the present, ladies. Let's do this!" She moves to slip into the house through the window. She gets her head through the open window, but she's wearing a bright-yellow fanny pack around her waist and it catches on the window frame as she tries to swing her legs in behind her. "Crap," she mutters. Sarah steps back on the deck, unclips her fanny pack from her waist and tosses it to me. I smile at her as I catch it and then look down to attach it around my waist. Seconds later, the deck gives out an incredibly loud groan.

We all freeze, and my eyes dart around. "Shit, shit, shit!" I mutter under my breath and pray that the deck is not succumbing to the weight of the snow.

Ellen is still the only one in the house, and she steps away from the window. The three of us still on the deck move from the open window and into the shadows. We all stay completely still, listening and waiting to see if the noise attracts the attention of the guard. Sure enough, it does.

The guard peers out the windows of one of the many doors that lead from the main house to the deck and then tentatively opens the door and takes a small step out onto the deck. There is an overhang above the door so the area right in front of the door is fairly clear of snow, but beyond that, he would have to walk in knee-deep snow. There is a light over the door and I can see his face, but we are all in the shadows and I'm pretty sure he cannot see any of us. He shines his flashlight around a bit, and it reflects off all the new-fallen snow. Apparently, he sees nothing of concern. He clips his light back onto his belt and turns to go back inside.

I breathe an almost audible sigh of relief as he grabs for the door handle, but just then, the deck emits another even larger groan. This causes him to pause and again reach for his flashlight, but the deck begins to give way. It seems like it crumples in slow motion, and I feel it weaken beneath my feet while looking around frantically for something to grab on to. There's nothing but mounds of snow everywhere. Kat and Sarah are both standing slightly closer to the house than I am, and they're both out of reach. I look up and see fear displayed across their shocked faces before I start to fall away from them.

I know the deck hangs over the cliff behind the house. As I fall, I wait to feel my body crash into the rocks below. Instead, I slam into a large, steep snowbank and roll down the side of it until I smash into the fragile ice that has formed on the edge of the river. By some miracle, I missed the rocks beneath the deck. It is only December and the fast-moving river has yet to totally freeze over. In fact, I can hear running water very nearby. I'm in pain and begin to panic as I try to get to my feet only to hear the thin ice starting to crack under my weight. In a matter of seconds, my left foot and then my right punch through the thin ice. Both my legs plunge into the freezing cold water.

I look back up toward the house but can only see darkness except the light outside the door from which the security guard appeared. I yell out but can hear nothing over the sound of the river. The riverbed on which I fell is very steep and covered in deep, deep snow. I cannot see any way to scramble back up toward the house. Unable to go back the way that I came, I set my sights on the opposite side of the river, which appears to be relatively flat. I start to wade through the icy water, which becomes deeper and starts to seep over the top of my Sorel snow boots and eventually soaks through my ski pants. The freezing water stings against my skin, and I know that hypothermia could kick in quickly even though the top of my body is still above water. The current of the river is not incredibly strong, but it still forces me slightly downstream away from the Schuyler House as I wade for the opposite bank. The river has got to be at least one hundred feet wide, and when I finally reach the opposite bank, I drag myself out of the water and up onto the snowy shore.

Once I reach a standing position, I turn to look back across the river. I can see lights from the Schuyler House, and I'm shocked to see how far away it seems. I scream out for my friends again and again but hear nothing but the roaring sound of the river running past me. My gaze darts back and forth along the riverbank looking for any sign of life. I'm near the point of hysteria and I step one foot back into the water, desperate to reunite with my friends. My feet are numb and the snow has started to fall even more heavily. Gradually, I come to grips with the fact that there's no way I can get back there.

At this point, I'm shivering uncontrollably. It occurs to me that I need to get warm, and fast. I turn away from the river and see nothing but trees all around me. Under different circumstances, I might even say it was pretty.

With no other choice, I head off into the trees. It's immensely difficult to walk in the deep snow, but the exertion may be my only hope to stave off the hypothermia.

CHAPTER SIX

I struggle through the woods for at least ten minutes before I see light up ahead. I continue to walk toward the light, and a small one-story house becomes visible. As I walk toward the house, I calculate that it now has to be close to one o'clock on Christmas morning. Finally, I reach the driveway that leads up to the house and am pleasantly surprised to find it's been plowed recently. This makes the walk up to the house seem effortless compared to plodding through the woods. My persistent shivering brings some urgency to get inside the house and out of my soaking wet clothes.

The house is totally dark except for a light over the front door, which prompts me to instead work my way over to a carport I can see on the far side of the house. When I reach the carport, I make note of the old, black Ford F-150 pickup truck parked beneath it before heading for the side door to the house. I give the door a tug, and it opens into a tidy mudroom/laundry room off the main house. When I step inside, I'm overcome with the feeling of warm air hitting my face. I close the door behind me and hastily pull off my gloves and reach down to unzip my wet ski coat. That's when I notice Sarah's yellow fanny pack is still fastened snugly around my waist. The sight of it immediately sends a wave of panic through me. I know I need to focus on getting out of my wet clothes and I need to get warm as quickly as possible, but I have absolutely no idea where my friends are nor any idea what happened to Kat and Sarah when the deck collapsed.

I lean down and unclip the fanny pack from my waist and set it on the floor carefully, kick off my big Sorel winter boots and start to peel off my snow pants, ski jacket, down vest, and my three layers of polypropylene long underwear. As I'm doing this, I look around the room and notice some large flannel shirts strung on a laundry line in the far corner of the room and a pile of neatly folded towels on top of the dryer. I lean over and grab two towels off the dryer, wrap one around my head and use the other to dry myself off. I grab two flannel shirts off the clothesline and slip them over my cold body. I reach into a nearby laundry basket and dig out a pair of jeans and a pair of wool socks. The jeans must belong to a heavyset man; they hang off my slender five-foot-eight frame. I don't see a belt lying around, so I use a few clothespins to keep the jeans from sliding off. The socks totally reek, but I'm not really in a position to be picky so I slip them over my ice-cold feet.

Once I'm dressed in dry clothes, I reach down to gather my jacket and the fanny pack. I set the fanny pack on top of the dryer and begin to search the pockets of my jacket for my cell phone. I hope that one of my friends has tried to call or sent me a text. I pray that Kat and Sarah survived the deck collapse uninjured and that they, along with Ellen, were able to escape safely back to the Tahoe on the snowmobiles. At this point, the fact that we failed to reach the art is the least of my concerns; I just want to talk to my friends so I know they are all okay. And the guard… Oh God, I think to myself. *I hope he is okay too.*

I find my iPhone zipped into the inside pocket of my ski coat, and it's moist to the touch, not a good sign. I fiddle with the phone and I start to hyperventilate when I realize it's totally dead. The salesman who sold me the ski coat went on and on about how it was both waterproof and breathable. I guess that doesn't hold true when one wades through an icy river. I curse under my breath until I remember Sarah's fanny pack. I reach over and grab it off the dryer and dump out all the wet contents onto the top. I start to curse again. Her cell phone is not in the fanny pack; she must have stuffed it in one of her coat pockets like I did. I take a quick inventory of the items piled up on the dryer. There's about $500 in cash in various denominations, Sarah's driver's license, a credit card, a small flashlight, a Swiss Army knife, and a pack of gum. I pack everything back in the fanny pack and decide it's time to get moving.

I grab a nicely folded pillowcase off the dryer and stuff all my wet clothes into it. Shoes—I need shoes. I briefly consider putting my Sorel boots back on, but they are soaked and a nice puddle is forming around them on the floor. I look around the laundry room and spot a pair of women's rubber boots beneath the line of flannel shirts, so I decide to slip those on instead. I lean down and pick up my wet boots and the pillowcase full of clothes and look around the room for keys to the old Ford F-150 parked out in the carport. I don't see anything that looks like car keys so I'm hoping they are in the ignition of the truck—that is pretty typical in this neck of the woods.

I head out the door where I came in and walk over to the driver's side of the truck, slowly open the door and reach down to feel for the keys. Bingo, they're in the ignition, just as I had hoped.

I'm about to try to fire up the truck when another idea occurs to me. The house sits on a small hill and, as a result, the driveway slopes down toward the road. The driveway has been plowed pretty recently, so it's possible I can let the truck roll down the hill somewhat before starting it. This would certainly reduce the likelihood of waking up the truck's owner when the engine turns over. I shift the truck in neutral, and it starts to roll backward slowly out of the carport. I can hear the tires crunching on the new snow, and the truck keeps rolling for about fifty yards but then comes to a complete stop as the driveway begins to level out down near the road. I shift the car back into park and grab hold of the keys while saying a quick prayer for the truck to start. It fires up right away, and I waste no time throwing it in reverse and backing out onto the road.

As soon as I'm a few hundred yards away from the house, I look down to see if the truck is in four-wheel drive, and once I am sure it is, I lean over to crank the heat to full blast. I curse as I am greeted with a blast of cold air since the truck's engine has yet to warm up. Heated seats would be nice but the truck is way too old to have them seats. After I finish berating the truck that, I note to myself, is kindly serving as my getaway car, I realize I've reached an intersection and have no idea where I am. For no particular reason, I decide to turn right. The snow is still coming down incredibly hard, and the visibility is horrible so I creep along at a snail's pace. The truck's headlights reflect off the falling snow and shine back into my face, but I don't really have any choice but to keep driving. I need to get away from the house with the carport, and I want to find my way back to Chicken Foot Road where we left Ellen's Tahoe.

Before long, I reach a stop sign where the road I am on intersects with a more major road that has been plowed very recently. Since I took a right at the last intersection, this time I decide to take a left. Fortunately, the heat in the car is starting to kick into high gear and my brain is starting to thaw out somewhat. For lack of a better plan, I will keep driving until I can figure out where the hell I am and then hopefully set about trying to find the Tahoe. If I had to guess, it's been over an hour since the deck collapsed and I plunged into the river. If Ellen, Sarah, and Kat survived the deck's collapse unscathed, they should be able to get back to the Tahoe by snowmobile in about thirty minutes. If the Tahoe is gone when I finally reach it, at least I will know that they made it out all right.

I drive for another fifteen or so minutes and come to a stop sign where the road I'm on runs into Route 29A. This is very good; I know Route 29A. Chicken Foot Road is off Route 29A. I don't have the best sense of direction and the old truck certainly doesn't have a GPS navigation system, but while we planned the Schuyler House burglary, I spent hours poring over maps of the area surrounding the estate. I know that we left the SUV east of the Schuyler House and traveled northwest on the snowmobile trail to reach the estate. I also know that the river into which I plunged runs roughly north to south. With that, I deduce that if I head east on Route 29A, I should run into Chicken Foot Road, assuming I can find it in this weather. I do have one thing going for me though: the house on the corner of Chicken Foot Road and Route 29A was inundated with Christmas decorations when we passed it earlier this evening in the Tahoe. There had to be at least ten thousand white Christmas lights encircling the house and nearly every tree in the large front yard. In case that was not enough, the house also has a giant blowup pig adorned with red bows in the front yard.

I crawl along Route 29A in the heavy snow for what feels like at least an hour and start to worry that I've missed Chicken Foot Road. It's possible that the guy with the crazy Christmas decorations turns off all his lights after midnight or something. Without those lights, I could have easily missed the turnoff. Just as I am about to turn around and head back the other way, I see the beacon of white Christmas lights off in the distance.

As I approach the well-lit house, I slow the truck down and turn off Route 29A and onto Chicken Foot Road. If it's still there, the Tahoe should be about a quarter mile down the road. Not surprisingly, Chicken Foot Road is in much worse shape than Route 29A. In fact, I would guess that it has not been plowed since we drove down it in the Tahoe a few hours earlier. I think I can make out a set of car tracks, but it's hard to judge how recent they are.

Even in four-wheel drive, the old Ford is really struggling in the deep snow and I'm afraid it will get stuck. Reluctantly, I decide I would probably be better off walking the quarter mile up the road to see if the Tahoe is still where we left it. I carefully maneuver the Ford F-150 slightly farther up the road so that it's away from the spotlight of the over-decorated house and is no longer easily visible from Route 29A. I've left tire tracks in the snow, but they should be covered by fresh snow in a matter of minutes.

I put the truck in park and am about to kill the engine when it occurs to me that I am wearing nothing but two huge flannel shirts and a pair of enormous grandma jeans, not exactly ideal attire for trekking a quarter mile through knee-deep snow. I rummage around behind the seats of the truck and find an old Carhartt jumpsuit like the ones you see construction workers wear when they have to work outside in really cold weather. It's filthy and way too big for me, but it will keep me warm. I kick off my borrowed rubber boots and wrangle myself into the jumpsuit. I slip back into the rubber boots, grab the flashlight out of Sarah's fanny pack, kill the engine and jump down onto the snowy road.

I'm grateful Sarah's flashlight still works even after it went for a swim in the river with me. I shine it up Chicken Foot Road and start to walk toward the Tahoe. It's very slow going. The combination of the deep snow and the bulky jumpsuit make it incredibly difficult for me to walk. In a matter of minutes, I am seriously sweating. After about thirty minutes, the beam of the flashlight reflects off something in the distance, and after a few more minutes, I'm able to make out the sign for the snowmobile trail a few hundred yards ahead.

A huge wave of relief hits me when I see that the Tahoe is gone, but as I get a bit closer, I spot one of our snowmobiles ditched in the snowbank at the side of the road. That doesn't make sense. Kat, Ellen, and Sarah would have needed two snowmobiles to get back to the Tahoe. I start to run through the possibilities in my head, and the only explanation that I can think of is that they took one snowmobile with them in case the Tahoe got stuck in the snow but decided not to waste the time to load them both up on the trailer. It doesn't really seem to add up, but I'm sure they were anxious to get as far away from Schuyler House as quickly as they could. I'm anxious to get out of there too and turn to start the slow walk back to the truck. I just wish I had a damn phone so that I could try and reach my friends and let them know I'm okay.

The walk back to the truck goes a little faster than the walk in since I now have my footsteps to follow. The snow hasn't yet totally covered the trail that I broke on the way in. Nonetheless, I'm happy when I see the Ford F-150 parked up ahead and I pick up my pace. I'm about fifty yards from the truck when I see the telltale flashing blue lights. I watch in horror as a cop slows on Route 29A and turns onto Chicken Foot Road. I am a complete sitting duck when he shines his bright white cop light on the Ford F-150 and then directs it up the road in my direction. The light is blinding and its reflection off the snow lights up Chicken Foot Road like it's the bright of day. I reach up to shield my eyes.

The cop steps out of the car and my body goes numb with fear. My first instinct is to run but I realize that is ridiculous. It would take me at least thirty seconds to make it through the deep snow to the nearest patch of trees. For the cop, it would be like shooting fish in a barrel. Instead, I take a few deep breaths and walk unsteadily toward him. I raise my hand and give him a friendly wave like we're two acquaintances greeting one another at the neighborhood hardware store.

He walks toward me and we meet alongside the F-150. I give him a long look and try to gauge whether he's here to capture me or thinks I'm just a plain old stranded motorist. "Good evening sir," I say as confidently as I can.

"Evening ma'am. No one in his or her right mind should be out on a night like this. Everything okay?"

He doesn't appear like he's readying to cuff me and toss me into the back of his SUV. I let out a sigh of relief and my brain starts racing. I feel I need to explain why I am out in the middle of a snowstorm in the middle of the night. "Um, yeah, everything's fine. Our dog went missing just after the snow started coming down. We looked everywhere and were really starting to worry because of the storm. I walk him on this road a lot so I thought maybe he came this way. But, my husband just texted to say he found the dog," I explain and hope I don't sound too rambly and nervous.

"Well, glad to hear he's okay. Can I escort you home?"

Oh, shit, I think to myself. Think fast Pearson. "Um, well, that's very kind of you but I'm sure you've got more important things to do in a storm like this. Plus, my husband knows where I am and he can come help me if I get stuck or something," I reply.

"Alrighty then. You stay safe. Oh, and, Merry Christmas," he says.

"Merry Christmas to you too, sir. Have a good evening."

I climb in the cab of the Ford F-150 and stare in awe as the cop turns around and heads back to Route 29A. That was a little too close for comfort, I think to myself. I fire up the truck, eager to get the hell out of there. It's hard to tell exactly where the road ends and the ditch alongside it begins; I do my best to stay in the center of the road as I work to turn the truck around. The last thing I need is to get stuck in the snow. After completing an at least eight-point turn, the truck is finally facing back toward Route 29A.

I work my way back on Route 29A toward Vermont. Just then, reality of my situation starts to set in and I am utterly amazed that cop didn't haul me away. I mean, I'm driving around in a stolen truck only a short distance from the Schuyler House. Surely the security guard has called in the attempted burglary by now. It will be nothing short of a miracle if I can get out of the area. The fact that it is Christmas Eve and we're in the midst of a major snowstorm has turned out to be a distinct disadvantage—the roads are virtually empty so any vehicle out on the road sticks out like a major sore thumb.

CHAPTER SEVEN

I glance down at my watch and cannot believe that it's almost five a.m. "Holy crap," I mutter as I reckon that the owner of the truck I'm driving is likely to wake up soon and notice his vehicle is no longer parked under his carport.

I've managed to cover a fair number of miles since I left Chicken Foot Road, especially given the road conditions. I just turned onto Route 8 and know that I'm roughly heading in the direction of Vermont, although I'd like to touch base with my friends and ditch my stolen truck before I cross the state line. Before I have time to further contemplate my predicament, the truck's low fuel light starts to blink, causing me to start cursing again. Based on the last sign I saw, I should be within a few miles of Cantonville, a small town through which Route 8 passes. I realize that the likelihood there's a gas station in Cantonville that happens to be open at five o'clock on Christmas morning is pretty slim, but I keep my fingers crossed nonetheless.

Finally, I enter Cantonville, and it's a stretch to even call it a town. There isn't even a traffic light and the one and only gas station is closed; however, I do spot the neon sign for a small motor inn just as I reach the far edge of town. For lack of any better option, I steer the truck toward the motor inn. I opt to follow the signs directing me to overflow parking around back rather than grabbing a spot in front of the inn. The overflow parking lot for the inn is empty except for two large motor coaches parked in the back left corner of the lot. I park the Ford as far as I can from the motor coaches and walk slowly toward the dimly lit back entrance of the inn. I try the back door. It's unlocked and leads into a small room with coin laundry machines and a small sitting room off to the right.

When I step inside, I can hear voices coming from the sitting room, and it sounds like there's a TV on in the background. I walk past the laundry machines and poke my head in the sitting room. I'm surprised to see two large men sitting in the corner sipping coffee from Styrofoam cups. They are facing the TV and their backs are to me so they don't seem to notice I've entered the room. I take a quick look around before ducking back into the laundry room area.

It's really warm in the laundry area of the inn, and even though I have pretty much thawed out by now, the warmth still feels really good. I have some time to kill before the gas station opens so I slide into one of the plastic chairs along the wall opposite the laundry machines. I stare at the machines in front of me and get the idea to toss my still-wet clothes into one of the dryers. It would enable me to get out of the ridiculous outfit I'm wearing and into clothes more suitable for the weather. My wet clothes are still in the truck so I jump out of my chair and head back out into the parking lot, where I grab the pillowcase with my clothes and my Sorel boots off the floor of the truck. I dig around in the ashtray to see if I can find a few quarters for the dryer. Bingo.

I walk back to the laundry room and toss my wet pile of clothes and boot liners into one of the dryers and insert my quarters.

Once my clothes start spinning around in the dryer, I slump in a nearby chair and just stare at them as they go round and round. I'm thoroughly exhausted, but my mind starts to race as gradually I replay the events of the horrific evening.

After a while, I tune in to the conversation the two men in the lobby are having. From what I can gather, they're the drivers for the buses parked out in the lot, and their passengers are a large group of skiers from a Jewish group in New York City. It sounds like they were supposed to head back to the city yesterday but got stranded by the storm and are both carrying on about how much it royally sucks to be stranded on Christmas morning. The skiers are due to emerge from their rooms any minute now, and the goal is to hit the road before the sun comes up. Apparently, the drivers are not Jewish because they both seem extremely bent out of shape at the possibility of missing Christmas morning with their families. I assume the inn is close to Gore Mountain, one of the larger ski areas in the area, which means we should be within three hours of New York City.

My eyes wander up to the TV screen in the room, and I mindlessly watch a *Seinfeld* rerun as I wait for my clothes to dry. Eventually, the episode ends and a local female news anchor appears on the screen. I pay attention vaguely to what she's saying, but my eyes nearly pop out of their sockets when a photo of the Schuyler House appears on the screen behind her. I abruptly sit up in my chair and crane my neck to try to hear what she's saying over the sound of the dryer. I can't help but notice that the two bus drivers have stopped talking and are both glancing up at the TV screen too. I reach down and clench the sides of my chair and hold my breath as the news anchor begins to speak.

"And now to breaking news…Two people were killed early this morning in an apparent botched Christmas Eve burglary at the Schuyler House. Police responded to a 911 call around one o'clock this morning and encountered a conscious but severely injured male security guard and two deceased females. The females' bodies were discovered in the ravine behind the house. Police haven't declared a cause of death for the two victims, but did say that they, along with the guard, were likely on the back deck of the house when it apparently collapsed under the weight of the snow. Police have not provided any additional details at this point, and it is not known if others were involved.

"Now on to the weather and an update on the storm that is walloping the region. Tom, is there an end in sight?"

The camera moves over to a lanky weatherman standing in front of a map. Holy fucking shit. I feel my throat constrict and feel like I might get sick. I close my eyes and take a few deep breaths. "Fuck! Fuck!" I say under my breath. How the hell did this happen?

My brain goes into total overdrive as I try to run through exactly what the news anchor said. I'm ninety-nine percent sure that she said two females were found, not three. I flash back to the moment the deck collapsed and try to put the pieces together. Ellen was definitely inside the house when the deck gave way, so that must mean that Kat and Sarah... Oh, God, it must mean that the two bodies they found in the ravine are Kat and Sarah... The urge to vomit overtakes me, and I jump from my seat and hurl into a nearby wastebasket.

Back in my chair, the next emotion to run through me is guilt. Why did I survive the fall when the deck crumbled but not Kat and Sarah? I mean, I was standing within a few feet of them when the deck gave way. It just doesn't make any sense. I do, however, feel a slight glimmer of hope at the possibility that Ellen was able to escape unharmed. The newscaster made no mention of a third female, dead or alive. The more I think about it, that would explain why I saw only one snowmobile ditched in the snowbank when I went back to Chicken Foot Road—there was only one snowmobile because only Ellen escaped from Schuyler House and emerged from the forest where we left the SUV.

My breathing is ragged as I try to digest the news. We knew what we did was fraught with risk, but I always framed that risk as risk of getting caught. One of us dying in the course of a burglary? That most certainly never crossed my mind. And God, what a freaking fluke accident that the deck collapsed just at that exact moment. If it had collapsed a few minutes earlier, or even a few minutes later, Kat and Sarah would most likely still be alive.

I stare into space. Obviously, there isn't anything I can do for Sarah and Kat at this point. I have no idea where Ellen is, and since my iPhone is totally dead, she has no way to reach me. I'm sure as hell not going to ask to use the inn's phone to try and reach her. That would be like sending up a flare to the police. I just need to get my hands on a cell phone, I think to myself while also realizing that I don't even have Ellen's number committed to memory. Her number, just like everyone else's, is saved in my contacts, which doesn't do me a hell of a lot of good right now.

One of the bus drivers sneezes, drawing my attention back to the other room. My eyes wander up to the TV where the female newscaster is back on and is now reminding viewers about the fire hazards associated with Christmas lights and candles. Merry fucking Christmas.

Slowly, I confront the reality that I cannot sit in this laundry room forever. I need to figure out where the hell I'm going to go from here, and I need to figure it out soon. It won't be much longer before the rightful owner of the Ford wakes up and realizes his truck is missing.

Obviously, one option is to hop back in the stolen truck and try to make it back to Vermont. I could gather up some of my belongings and try and find a place to hide out for a while. The newscaster seemed to imply that the police were still in the dark about any potential accomplices of the Schuyler House burglary, so this leads me to believe there isn't a major manhunt (or in this case a *woman*hunt) underway. I may be cocky, but I'm pretty confident that it's going to take even the sharpest cop some time to connect the dots between Kat, Sarah, Ellen, and me. It is not like Ellen and I left business cards at the scene, and I don't think there are any obvious clues that link the four of us together. Sure, we were all friends and we spent a good amount of time together, but we never discussed the burglaries in emails or text messages and we certainly didn't share our "hobby" with the people around us. In fact, the only person outside the four of us—aside from Olivier, of course—who even knew what we've been up to is Kat's husband Todd and, to some extent, good old Jake.

Nonetheless, I rule out trying to make it to Vermont. First off, I don't have a solid source of transportation. I don't want to risk driving that stolen truck for much longer, and it's not like I can walk out in front of the inn and hail a cab—I'm in the middle of nowhere! So that means I need a Plan B… I start to consider my alternatives when the beep of the dryer interrupts my thoughts.

I gather up my warm clothes and head toward the lobby to search for a ladies' room or someplace where I can change out of my flannel shirt ensemble and back into my ski pants and parka. I search around the various downstairs rooms of the hotel, and all I can find is some sort of maid's closet off the lobby. For lack of a better option, I duck in there, pull the string to turn on the light and find myself face-to-face with shelves full of toilet paper and industrial cleaning supplies. I kick off the rubber boots, slide the now dry liners back in my Sorel boots and quickly change my clothes. I reach down and gather the flannel shirts and the too-large jeans off the floor and look around for a place to stuff them in the closet before deciding I'm probably better off just putting the old clothes back in the truck. I stuff the clothes under my arm and slip back out of the closet.

It's at this point that I realize that I really have to pee, and my earlier search turned up no bathroom in the lobby of the small hotel. With no other immediate alternative, I head back out into the dark parking lot, toss the clothes in the back of the cab and then squat to pee behind the truck. I leave a big yellow stain in the snowbank, make a little snowball to use as toilet paper (a handy trick I learned while winter camping when I was in college) and start to walk back to the hotel lobby.

I get about halfway there when I see the two bus drivers coming out of the hotel heading toward their coaches in the back of the parking lot. One of them turns to me and says, "Ya better get your stuff. We're hitting the road in fifteen minutes. Hoping to make it back into the city by eleven o'clock." I stop dead in my tracks and watch them continue walking toward the buses.

Suddenly, Plan B becomes crystal clear to me. I'm going to leave the stolen truck parked behind the hotel and join the

Jewish skiers aboard the buses bound for New York. I cannot think of a better place in the world to hide out than New York, and it just so happens that the Hatshepsut Consulting safe deposit box is located at a bank in the middle of the city. That means I'll have access to more cash. Plus, I'm dressed the part in my ski pants and ski jacket. The fact that there are two motor coaches means the ski group is fairly big so hopefully I can easily blend in, especially if everyone is bundled up in winter clothes.

As I watch the drivers start up the buses and then come around to open up the cavernous luggage compartments, I consider moving the Ford to a lot across the street from the hotel just in case the police discover the stolen truck before the bus of skiers reaches New York. The cops could put two and two together and speculate that I ditched the truck and hopped on one of the ski buses, but I figure it's not worth it. The likelihood of them finding the truck and identifying it as stolen in the next four hours is extremely slim especially because the truck is parked behind the hotel and the license plate is nearly covered in snow.

I walk back into the hotel, buy a bottle of water and a package of cheese crackers from the vending machine in the laundry room, and then head back out to the buses. I do my best to blend in with the skiers starting to filter out of the hotel and toward the waiting coaches. I figure walking out with them will make it less obvious that I don't have any luggage; most notably, I don't have a ski bag. I climb up into the first bus and sit down in a window seat about halfway back. The bus fills up quickly, and eventually a young woman plunks down into the aisle seat next to me. She doesn't seem to be with anyone else and doesn't so much as glance at me before slipping on her Beats headphones and pulling a book out of her bag. Perfect, I think to myself. Doesn't look like she will be a talker. Everyone on the bus seems pretty groggy given the early hour; half the bus's riders are dozing off before we even leave the hotel parking lot.

I'm suddenly and completely overwhelmed with exhaustion. I close my eyes, and warm tears wander down my face as I think about Sarah and Kat.

Eventually, I must doze off because when I open my eyes again, we're pulling off Rte. 87 south of Albany. That means we've probably been on the road for more than two hours. The bus makes its way to a McDonald's not far from the highway, and people file off to grab breakfast and use the restroom.

After the pit stop, where I grab some food for myself, I just stare out the window and sip my coffee as we continue to roll south on I-87 toward the Big Apple. My mind is totally numb. I know I need to figure out what I'm going to do when we actually arrive in New York, but I'm having a really hard time thinking about anything except for the events of the previous evening. I truly cannot believe that two of my very best friends and long-time partners in crime are dead. *Dead.* I repeat the word, letting it sink in.

For so many years, the four of us treated our escapades like a game. We never really acknowledged or admitted, at least I didn't, that what we were doing was seriously dangerous. In retrospect, I cannot help but think what idiots we were. At least, I wish we'd had the sense to stop doing it after the first few times. Our luck was bound to run out at some time…

Finally, we make our way across the famous George Washington Bridge, and it occurs to me that I have no idea where the bus will eventually stop to drop us all off. The Manhattan skyline comes into view, and I feel the bus start to slow down. Even under the circumstances, I can't help but admire the sea of the towering skyscrapers. Their massive glass and metal facades shimmer in the morning sunlight and its beautiful. The bus turns off onto Route 278 which means we must be headed to Brooklyn. No surprise there.

The bus pulls to a stop about twenty minutes later in front of the Park Slope Jewish Center, an imposing yellow brick building right near Prospect Park. Everyone files off the bus slowly and gathers around as the drivers open the luggage holds and start to pull out suitcases and ski bags. I stand with all of the other passengers and pretend to wait for my nonexistent luggage while assessing my surroundings. I check my watch, and it is almost ten o'clock. The sky is a crisp blue and it's very cold. Luckily, there is virtually no wind so the cold is not as biting as it could be. Instinctively, I wrap my arms around my body and bounce from foot-to-foot to keep warm. Most of the skiers appear to grab their luggage and then head into the Jewish Center, so casually I follow a group inside in hopes of finding a ladies' room and possibly a computer I can use for a few minutes.

The Center is massive. After I use the bathroom, I wander down a long hallway lined with doorways leading to what look like classrooms. I try a few of the knobs, but all of the doors appear to be locked until I reach one near the end of the hall that's ajar. I poke my head in the open door and see what must be some sort of children's library room. There are rows of shelves packed with books and small tables and chairs scattered around the room. I step in and peek around a few of the bookshelves and find what I am looking for—a row of computers. The computers sit on desks made for someone half my size, but I pull out a pint-size chair and sit down at one of them. I'm sure someone is going to come in and kick me out any minute so I work quickly. First, I log on to my Gmail account and go straight to my contacts to find Ellen's cell number. Next, I log on to my Skype account and dial her number. My heart is racing as her phone starts to ring, and I'm crestfallen when it goes to voice mail. I hang up without leaving a message, log out of Gmail and Skype, climb out of the miniature chair and head back out into the long hallway to find the nearest exit.

Since the Center is located in the heart of Brooklyn, there should be a plethora of subway stations close by so I just begin to walk, figuring I'll bump into a subway station pretty quickly. Before too long, I find myself outside the Grand Army Plaza Station. When I step inside, I'm happy to find that it is a good bit warmer inside the station than it was outside. I lower the hood of my coat and look around for a MetroCard kiosk. Once I find the kiosks, I dig a twenty-dollar bill out of Sarah's fanny pack, feed it into the kiosk and wait for the machine to spit out my MetroCard. I grab my card and walk toward the entry gates, happy to see that the Four Train runs through this station.

I've been to New York enough times to know this train heads straight into the heart of Manhattan and up the Eastside.

I walk down to the tracks for the Four Train, and while I'm waiting decide to head to the Metropolitan Museum of Art. The train will stop nearby since it's on the Eastside, and it will be a good, warm place to wander while I figure out what the hell I'm going to do. I laugh to myself as I consider the fact that going to an art museum is a tiny bit ironic given my current circumstances, but somehow, this plan calms me.

That is, until I realize a few minutes later that it's Christmas Day and the Met will most certainly be closed. Shit. I need somewhere to sit and think—ideally, somewhere warm.

CHAPTER EIGHT

The Four Train heads north soon after it crosses the East River. I ride it for a few stops and decide to jump off near City Hall and catch an uptown Two Train. I hop on the Two and take it up along the west side of Central Park before getting off at 96th Street to transfer and take the One Train up to 116th Street near Columbia University.

As soon as I exit the station, the cold air slams me, so I pull the hood of my coat up over my head and set off down the street. I spent a lot of time in this area of the city when I was in college and dated a woman who attended Columbia. I wander along the once-familiar streets until I come across the old Newton Hotel and the neighboring Gaslight Diner. The old Newton Hotel looks just as seedy as it did ten plus years ago, and my guess is it still primarily accommodates hourly cash-paying guests as long as the proper deposit is made.

It's not quite noon at this point so it's probably still too early to try to check into the hotel. The Gaslight Diner appears to be open even though it's Christmas; I figure I will go in there and have some more coffee and maybe order a small nibble. I make a beeline for the long lunch counter that lines the back of the restaurant. The place is nearly empty, and I climb up on one of the stools, take off my ski parka and rest it on the stool beside me. I feel a little out of place in ski pants in the middle of Manhattan especially because there is absolutely no snow on the ground, but I don't have a lot of options at this point, and honestly, I'm way too exhausted to really care.

The waitress working the counter scurries over and slaps a multipage plastic menu down on the counter in front of me. She's in her early twenties with bleach-blond frizzy hair and is wearing a nametag that reads "Irene."

"Mornin'. Coffee?" she mumbles.

"Sure, black," I croak.

She grabs my coffee cup and, in one smooth motion, flips it over and fills it. I smile a thank-you, and she wanders off to leave me to flip through the vast menu dotted with pictures of moist omelets, frothy milkshakes, and juicy hamburgers. I am surprised that the pictures make me hungry even though I had an Egg McMuffin just a few hours ago. I decide on a grilled cheese sandwich and tomato soup—comfort food seems fitting.

The waitress places a big glass of ice water in front of me. "Ready to order?"

I nod and give her my order, and she shuffles off to the next customer.

I take a long drink of water and then sip on my coffee like a zombie while I wait for my food. It occurs to me again that it's Christmas Day and two of my closest friends are spending Christmas morning in the morgue. I remember that Sarah's two boys are spending Christmas with their father in Maine, and I wonder if they've heard the news about their mother. Those poor boys, I think to myself just as the waitress places my grilled cheese and soup down in front of me. The soup is piping hot, and I dunk my sandwich into it like a little kid. I wish the diner had a TV so I could see if the news is reporting anything new on the events at Schuyler House.

I finish my meal and drain my coffee cup. I leave money on the counter, including a generous tip, pull on my coat and head toward the back of the diner in search of a ladies' room.

The door to the restroom opens just as I turn to grab some paper towels to dry my hands, and Irene walks in and gives me a faint nod of recognition. She's carrying a coat over her arm and has a cloth bag over her shoulder.

"Shift over?" I ask.

"Yeah, finally. Some way to spend Christmas, huh?" she says as she enters a stall.

I head out of the restroom and walk back across the diner toward the hostess stand, and suddenly I get an idea. I reach into Sarah's fanny pack, pull out a crisp hundred-dollar bill and tuck it into my hand as I head back outside. The cold air slams me in the face again, and I duck into a nearby doorway to wait for Irene to follow me outside. About three minutes later, she exits the diner and I approach her quickly.

"Hey," I yell, and she looks up. "Hold on, I have a question to ask you…"

She looks up at me curiously. "Oh, hi! What's up?"

I'm not exactly sure how to explain what I need. "Uhmm, I have a favor to ask you, no obligation."

"Okay," she says guardedly while looking me up and down.

"Will you check me into the hotel next door if I give you a hundred bucks?" She looks at me quizzically but doesn't say anything so I continue. "I need a safe place to sleep and I don't want my husband to find me. He's a cop and he is crazy."

I feel bad for lying, but she looks at me understandingly and nods. "Sure."

A smile of relief crosses my face, and I explain my game plan to her. "If it's okay, I will just follow you to the check-in desk and I'll hand you whatever cash you need to pay for the room and the deposit. They will probably ask to see your ID…You have one, right?"

She nods, and I continue. "Once they give you a room key, we can head up the elevator together, but as soon as we get upstairs, you can turn right around and leave. You don't have to come into the room or anything…I mean…"

She interrupts my rambling. "It's okay, you don't seem like a crazy person. I'm happy to help."

Yeah, I'm just *wanted*, I think to myself as we turn to enter the hotel.

The Newton is a serious dump. The lobby is brightly lit and adorned with only a ratty sofa, a few chairs and a few randomly placed fake plants. Irene and I make our way to the check-in desk, and the clerk grunts some sort of greeting.

"We need a room for the night," Irene says matter-of-factly.

"I need to see some ID," the clerk barks, and Irene hands over her driver's license.

The clerk pokes his computer for a bit and eventually looks up. "It'll be seventy-nine dollars plus tax, and I need a seventy-five-dollar deposit, cash only."

I hand Irene some cash, and she pays for the room and the deposit.

"Room 713," the clerk growls as he reaches his meaty hand over the counter to give Irene one of those plastic key cards. "Checkout is eleven o'clock, no exceptions," he says as he points us toward the elevator at the far side of the lobby.

We walk over to the elevators, and I hit the "Up" button. The ancient elevator takes forever to arrive, and I feel myself sweating under my ski clothes both because I am hot and because I am nervous as shit. When the elevator doors finally creak open, Irene and I both step into the elevator. I repeatedly push the button for the seventh floor, but it doesn't light up. Irene points to a sign that a room key is required to operate the elevator. She swipes the key card over a little sensor, and this time the number seven lights up when I press it. While the elevator creeps up toward the seventh floor I hand Irene a hundred-dollar bill, and she gives me the room key in exchange.

"Thanks for helping me out. You are free to leave now," I assure as the elevator stops at my floor.

"You're welcome," she says as I step off and the elevator doors close between us.

I slide the key in the lock for Room 713, push the door open and flip on a light. The room has hospital-green walls and shabby brown carpet and consists of a queen bed, a dresser with an old TV on top, and a wooden chair and desk. I poke my head into the bathroom; the fixtures and tile are dated, but it seems relatively clean. The room feels cold so I look around for the thermostat and crank up the heat before heading into the bathroom to take a quick shower. I'm ready for a nap; I barely slept on the bus and I'm totally beat.

CHAPTER NINE

I sleep hard for about two hours until an incredibly full bladder wakes me up. I'm still completely exhausted, but it's only late afternoon and I want to head back out to buy some supplies before I turn in for the night. I'm pretty confident that at least some stores in the neighborhood will be open even though it's Christmas Day. I'm in New York, after all—the city that never sleeps, not even on Christmas Day. I count the remaining cash in the fanny pack, bundle up in my ski clothes and head back out to the street.

First, I go to Duane Reade and buy a toothbrush and toothpaste, a sample size of shampoo (since the hotel is too cheap to provide it), some deodorant, a six-pack of Fruit of the Loom underwear with little flowers on them, a pack of ballpoint pens, and a notebook. Then I wander another block or so until I come across an electronics store with lots of flashing strobe lights in the front windows. It looks like the kind of place that sells cell phones, so I go inside.

Every inch of the walls in the store is covered with those pegboard displays. The store seems to carry about one hundred different makes and models of cell phone, and I nearly trip over a pile of boxes as I try to reach the area of the store where most of the cell phones are located. After scanning the incredible selection, I yank a mid-priced Motorola phone off the wall and go in search of the cashier. The store is totally empty, and the cashier is sitting on a stool watching a movie on his iPad. He stands up when I approach the counter, and I hand him the Motorola phone to ring up.

He takes a look at the phone. "Do you need a SIM card?" he asks. I stare back at him blankly, and he points to a wall of SIM cards next to his booth. "Cell phones don't work unless you have a SIM card," he explains patiently. "SIM cards hold information like the phone number and cell provider. Most people who come in here buy prepaid SIM cards. They can be topped up as needed. Basically, you just pay in advance for service so you don't have to mess with a plan from one of the big carriers."

"Oh." I try to digest all of this. "You said that each SIM card has its own phone number?" I ask, and he nods.

I walk over and scan the SIM card wall and grab two SIM cards off one of the pegs—one for me to use temporarily until I can get to the Apple store in the morning and the other one to use as a "clean" phone number I can give to Ellen. My goal is to visit the Hatshepsut safe deposit box in the morning to get some more money. I'm hopeful that Ellen will eventually make her way to New York and that she'll visit the safe deposit box too. After all, we set up the safe deposit box just for this type of emergency. Anyway, my plan is to leave Ellen a phone number in the safe deposit box so she knows how to reach me.

I pay for my new electronics and head back out to the street. I start to walk back toward the hotel, but on my way, I pass a small Chinese grocery store that appears to be open. I head in and am psyched to see a giant buffet bar steaming at the back of the store. I load up a take-away container with food, grab some plastic silverware and a six-pack of Sierra Nevada Pale Ale, pay the cashier and then continue toward the hotel.

When I get back to my palatial room at the Newton, I flip on the TV and surf the channels until I come across *Anderson Cooper 360* on CNN. I've always liked Anderson Cooper. I pull my new cell phone and SIM cards out of the bag and set them out on the desk. I rip open the package of the cell phone, extract the phone and plug it into the wall so that it can charge. Then I sit down at the well-worn desk and pick up one of the SIM card packages to read the instructions. I open one of the cards and insert it into my new cell phone as it charges. Then I open the second SIM card package and jot down the phone number associated with it. I label the card with the words "Ellen phone number" before slipping it into the inside pocket of my ski coat.

Once that's done, I pull out my Chinese take-out box and scarf down every last bite of food inside while sipping on one of the beers. Apparently, this running from the law stuff is causing me to have an amazing appetite. After I gorge myself on Chinese food, I pop open another beer and pick up my new cell phone. It's charged up somewhat, so I type in Ellen's phone number and hold my breath as it rings.

"Damn, Ellen, where are you?" I mutter when it goes to voice mail again. I stab the phone to end the call and sit back down at the small desk. I open the pack of pens and the notebook that I bought at Duane Reade and doodle on a piece of paper as I start to weigh my options.

I write *Option # 1: Stay in New York City*. I could stay in New York, but for a reason that I cannot pinpoint, I don't want to, so then I jot down *Option 2: Go back to Vermont*. I know I want to get back to Vermont eventually, but I know it's way too soon to even seriously contemplate that as an option. Not to mention the fact that I don't currently have a car at my disposal. That leads me to write *Option 3: Fly somewhere far away, ideally foreign*. But I quickly admit that Option 3 is totally stupid. I'm certainly not going to fly somewhere using my license as ID, and it would be way too risky to try to fly anywhere using Sarah's driver's license. I don't happen to have a passport on me so sneaking off to some foreign destination is also completely unrealistic at this point.

At this point I'm stumped, and I start to doodle some more until another option pops into my head. I write *Option 4: Washington, DC*. I can easily get there on the train or bus—check. I know and love the city since I lived there for many years after college—double check! DC is likely to be a tad warmer than New York—Option 4 seems like the clear winner, and after a little more doodling, I decide to head to DC sometime the next day before turning my attention to formulating my game plan for the next forty-eight hours.

First thing tomorrow morning, I'll go to the bank where we have the safe deposit box. From there, I will head to the Apple Store and get myself a laptop and new iPhone. Finally, I'll shop for a change of clothes and a couple of other supplies before I take off for DC… Now I just have to figure out the best way to get to DC. Amtrak is the first thing that comes to my mind, but I figure taking the Chinatown bus is probably a better idea. The Chinatown bus is dirt-cheap and seems like a good way to stay below the radar.

Once I've established my near-term game plan, I turn to a fresh page in the notebook so I can write a note to Ellen to leave in the Hatshepsut safe deposit box the next morning. I'm seriously counting on the fact that she made it out of Schuyler House uninjured and undetected. The limited news I've seen on the Schuyler House burglary makes no mention of her, so I have to assume she's on the run like me.

I start my note to her by writing the date at the top of the page, and this is enough to cause the tears to start. Pretty soon, I'm sobbing uncontrollably and have to go to the bathroom to get a Kleenex so that I can blow my nose. Eventually, my tears subside enough that I can start to write…

Dear Ellen,

I am completely and utterly beside myself with grief about what happened at Schuyler House. I am sure you know by now that Sarah and Kat are dead. God, I still cannot believe it. How the hell could something like that have happened? It's still all a blur and it all happened so fast. One second I was out on the deck next to Sarah and Kat and the next second I was in a giant snowbank on the side of the river. I tried so hard to get back up to the house but the snow was too deep and the riverbank was too steep.

I want to see you and talk to you so badly. I hope you find this note soon. I tried to call you but got voice mail. I will keep trying you but please call me at the number below the second you read this.

I am in NYC now but I plan to go to DC tomorrow. I pray that you are all right.

Love,

Mattie

I glance over at the "Ellen phone number" that I jotted down from the second SIM card and scribble it at the bottom of my note and then tuck the note into my ski coat.

I decide to try Ellen one more time before going to bed. Much to my disappointment, I get voice mail just like all the other times, but this time I decide to leave her a cryptic message. I pretend to be someone asking her to donate money to the biannual NPR fund drive and leave the "Ellen phone number" as the call back number. If she gets the message, I'm pretty sure she will figure out it's me—we both listen to NPR religiously, and we used to moan about their biannual fund drive during which they constantly interrupt the morning broadcast to plead for donations, promising that callers will be entered in a drawing for twenty free iPads.

I hang up and set the cell phone on the desk. I pull SIM card #1 out of the phone and stuff it inside my Chinese take-out container and toss it in the garbage. I've probably read too many James Patterson books; I am totally paranoid that if the police have Ellen's cell phone they will eventually trace it to the SIM card.

Before climbing into bed, I pull the second "clean" SIM card (the card with the "Ellen number") out of my ski coat and pop it into the Motorola phone. However, now that I have inserted the "clean" SIM card into the phone, I have absolutely no intention of using the Motorola phone again. I will just keep it charged and cross my fingers that Ellen either listens to my phony NPR voice mail or gets the note I plan to leave for her in the safe deposit box and eventually calls me.

I slip under the covers and turn out the light. I am completely exhausted but I cannot fall asleep. My mind just churns. It's like there's a little Indy race going on in my brain. I keep going over and over the events of the last twenty-four hours. Goddammit, we were so stupid, I say to myself. So, so stupid. The money and the thrill clouded our judgment. Who am I kidding, we let it completely shroud our judgment. And now Kat and Sarah are dead. I put my pillow over my face and scream into it. Then I fling the pillow onto the bed and punch it a few times.

I lay back down and stare at the ceiling. I vow I will never ever steal so much as a ketchup packet for the rest of my life. I'm going to become more law abiding than a nun.

CHAPTER TEN

After securing some breakfast, I check out of the hotel around eleven o'clock and cut through Morningside Park before turning toward Central Park. The bank where we have our safe deposit box is a Bank of America on the corner of Lexington and 43rd, so I cut through Central Park to get to the Eastside and then take the Five Train down to Grand Central Station. It's still really chilly, and the wind is blowing a lot more today than it was yesterday.

I get to the bank just as all the workers are starting to pour out of their offices for lunch and the bank is bustling with activity. Sarah and I are the ones who originally opened the safe deposit box for Hatshepsut Consulting, and I've visited the bank a few times since we opened the box so I know that I need to head to the desk in the back of the bank labeled Special Services. There are a few people in line at the desk ahead of me, so I try to patiently wait my turn but I'm super nervous, which makes me fidgety. My palms are all sweaty.

When I reach the desk, I indicate that I am here to access my safe deposit box, and the woman behind the desk picks up her phone to call someone. She looks up at me after she hangs up the phone. "Michael will be right out to greet you. Please have a seat," she says in a very high-pitched voice and points to a small seating area next to the desk.

Michael appears before I even have a chance to sit down and walks me into a small room off to the side of the main bank. He asks to see my ID and I hand him Sarah's license. He then directs me to sign a logbook before he escorts me into the area where the safe deposit boxes are located. Thankfully, I am still wearing my ski hat, and he doesn't seem to notice that I don't have curly red hair like the photo on the license.

Unlike the old days, a key is not required to open our box. Instead, we had to pick an eight-digit PIN, and in order to make ours easy to remember (and look up if necessary), we picked 1507-1457, the year in which Hatshepsut was born and the year in which she died (minus one in both cases to make the PIN a little less obvious). I enter our PIN, Michael enters the master PIN for the bank and this releases the safe deposit box from its hold.

He shows me to a small private room, and once the metal door locks behind me, I sit down and open the box. It has about $500,000 in cash plus four credit cards and four debit cards. All the credit and debit cards are in the name of the LLC that we set up—Hatshepsut Consulting. There should also be another $500,000 or so in the Hatshepsut Consulting's checking account. I take $100,000 in cash, one credit card and one debit card and leave the note I wrote for Ellen. The cash is mostly in hundred-dollar bills, but there are a few packs of twenty-dollar bills and it's pretty bulky. I spread as much cash as I can into the various internal and external pockets of my ski coat and jam the rest into Sarah's yellow fanny pack before summoning Michael so I can return the safe deposit box to the vault.

After I'm done at the bank, I walk up Lexington until I reach 57th Street and then cut over to Fifth Avenue. I pass throngs of tourists and well-clad shoppers and figure, based on my less than fashionable attire none of them would ever guess that I have a hundred grand in cash stuffed in my coat pockets. I stroll down Fifth Avenue until I get to the Apple Store on the northeast corner of Central Park. I go in, and less than thirty minutes later, walk out with a new MacBook Air and a new iPhone. From there I head to Patagonia, an outdoor clothing store known for their quality clothing, but also often referred to as "PataGucci" for the sometimes-exorbitant prices, and buy a small daypack with a bunch of external pockets plus a few pairs of warm socks.

My last stop is Macy's where I buy two pair of 7 For All Mankind jeans, a black leather belt, two new bras (since I only have a jog bra with me), two long sleeve T-shirts, and a black V-neck sweater. After the saleswoman at Macy's rings me up, I ask her if I can go back into the changing room and change into my new clothes. She smiles. "Of course, dear," she says and leads me back to the changing rooms. Once inside the changing room, I quickly peel off my layers of long underwear, exchange my fleece pants for a pair of jeans, swap out my jog bra for one of my new bras and slip into one of the T-shirts and my new sweater. I stuff my fleece pants, long-underwear tops, and jog bra along with the rest of my new clothes into my new daypack alongside my new laptop and head out of the store.

I walk a few blocks and duck into the first Starbucks I see so I can fire up my new computer and use the free Wi-Fi. Once I am online, I set up a new Gmail account, buy my ticket for the Chinatown bus to DC and start to poke around the Airbnb website for a place to stay in DC. Eventually, I settle on a small Airbnb apartment in the Logan Circle neighborhood and I send the host a request for a one-week stay beginning the next day.

Once that's done, I pack up my stuff and head back outside. I've still got some time to kill before my bus leaves. It is probably a good three or four miles from where I am to Chinatown but I decide to walk anyway. I've got nothing else to do and I could use some exercise.

It is just past eight o'clock when I reach Fifth Avenue and the street is a complete and utter zoo, packed with holiday tourists. I follow the hoards and wander by Rockefeller Center to see the Christmas tree and the ice skaters before continuing toward Chinatown.

The walk to Chinatown takes me about two hours including a little pit stop for a beer and some fish tacos. I arrive at the designated bus stop about fifteen minutes early. I'm surprised to see there's already a small queue of people lined up for the bus, and I take my place at the end of the line. I go to pull out my phone to scroll some news headlines, but the bus pulls up before I have a chance. The driver scans my e-ticket and I board and take a window seat about halfway back. The bus has Wi-Fi so, once I am seated, I pull out my laptop to see if I've heard from Bettie, the Airbnb host, and I'm relieved to see that she's confirmed my dates and can meet me the next day at three.

As the bus pulls away from the curb, I'm happy no one has taken the seat next to me. I take advantage of the extra room and curl up against the window to try and get some sleep during the trip, mindful that I have a hundred thousand dollars stuffed into my ski coat and fanny pack.

CHAPTER ELEVEN

It's still pitch black when we arrive in DC just before five o'clock, and the sun is showing no sign of rising any time soon. The bus drops us on the eastern side of Chinatown in DC, and the streets are totally deserted except for an occasional taxicab.

Once I get off the bus, I contemplate heading for Union Station but instead decide to walk toward Metro Center so I can take the train to Ronald Reagan National Airport, which is located just outside the city. The airport should already be hopping at this time of the morning and it seems like a good place to kill some time—the airport has free Wi-Fi, lots of options for food and clean restrooms—before I am scheduled to meet my Airbnb host later that afternoon.

When I get to Metro Center I go to one of the ticket kiosk machines and buy a SmartTrip card so I won't have to deal with paper tickets every time I want to ride the Metro. Once I have my SmartTrip card, I head down the escalator to the train platform, and an Orange Line train headed in the direction of National Airport pulls up a few minutes later. The train ride

is only about twenty minutes and the train is virtually empty
since it's still so early in the morning and I'm doing a reverse
commute—heading out of the city when most commuters are
headed in.

As soon as I get to the airport, I make a beeline to the ladies'
room—I was scared to use the toilet on the bus and I'm about
to burst plus I am dying to brush my teeth—and then I go in
search of something for breakfast. I buy a bacon, egg, and cheese
bagel sandwich and sit in a vacant row of chairs in front of big
windows that offer a nice view of the tarmac. I perch myself on
one of the chairs and stare out at the planes on the tarmac while
I slowly nibble on my breakfast sandwich. I eventually drag my
laptop out of my backpack and connect to the airport Wi-Fi.

I trawl through a bunch of news websites to see if there is
anything more on Schuyler House. The CNN site is dominated
by breaking news about a mega blizzard about to hit the Rockies
and the Midwest. I poke around some more but don't see
anything on the CNN site about Schuyler House so I navigate
to the Albany *Times-Union* website.

"Holy fucking shit!" I mutter a bit too loudly. The police
have already connected the dots and linked Ellen and me to
the attempted break-in at the Schuyler House. I am a bit taken
aback they made the connection so quickly. We were all really
careful and never exchanged emails or text messages about the
heists we planned. Guess we weren't as stealthy as we thought…
They must have uncovered something at Sarah's house linking
the four of us. We always used Sarah's house as our home base,
and obviously we got sloppy somewhere.

I skim the *Times-Union* article, and it refers to Ellen and me
as "people of interest" and has a photo of each of us, but mine
is from at least five years ago when I had much shorter hair and
Ellen's photo isn't all that current either. I note with some relief
that the article mentions Schuyler House but makes no mention
of any of our previous burglaries so I can only hope the police
never put together all the pieces of the puzzle.

I suddenly feel extremely exposed, like everyone in the
airport is looking at me. In reality though, I currently look

nothing like the picture, I'm five hundred miles away from Schuyler House and everyone at the airport is laser-focused on getting where they need to go. Plus, as of now, the story is only in the local paper. It's possible that CNN and the other big national media outlets will eventually pick it up, but hopefully it will be completely overshadowed by news of the imminent mega blizzard.

I shut my laptop and think about my sister Abby for the first time since the deck collapsed at Schuyler House. I wonder what she will think if and when she hears that I was part of an attempted art burglary. Abby is almost fifteen years older than me, and I haven't spoken to her more than once or twice since my mom died three years ago. She and I were never close growing up. The age difference had a lot to do with it, but Abby has resented me since the day I was born and has always tried her best to pretend that I don't exist. My mom was in her mid-forties when I was born and my father was well into his fifties—I was, without question, a surprise to all of them. Abby's resentment was likely magnified by the fact that my parents seemed to have more time for me than they did for her when she was young. My father spent her early childhood building his business and, once it was successful, he found time to go to my soccer games and swim meets when he'd rarely made it to hers. Anyway, Abby went to Georgia for college, married the son of a Baptist preacher and pretty much cut off all ties with me when I came out in high school. I was angry with her for so many years, but now our nonexistent relationship just makes me sad. I've always hoped that someday we would reconcile, but I guess that day is going to have to wait.

I'm jolted out of my daze when a large man in a tweed suit plunks down in the seat next to me, causing the entire row of chairs to wobble. I rub my eyes and check my watch and am surprised to see that it's already almost noon. I decide it's probably time for me to make my way back into the city. I take the Orange line from the airport to Farragut North which is right in the center of the business district and only a few blocks from the White House.

I walk north on Connecticut Avenue up through DuPont Circle and then, for no real reason, wander over toward Adams Morgan. It calms me to walk through the old neighborhoods I used to know so well. Halfway up Eighteenth Street in Adams Morgan, I cut over to Columbia Avenue and walk a few blocks until I come upon the running store where I used to buy all my running gear when I lived in DC. I wonder if I walked here subconsciously. On impulse, I open the door and go inside.

I browse the racks and racks of running clothes and scan the running shoes on display. Eventually, a salesman approaches and I ask to try on some shoes. He asks me a few questions about how much and how often I run and then asks me to walk toward the front door and back so that he can observe my gait. He thinks for a bit, disappears into the back room and quickly emerges with some shoes for me to try. I decide on a pair of pink-and-blue Saucony the salesman assures me will rock my running world. I grab some running tights and two pairs of running socks and follow him up to the register. While he's ringing me up, I take the shoes out of the box and tie them to the outside of my pack and stuff the tights and the socks into my now-full daypack.

I hand him the empty shoebox. "Do you mind recycling this for me?"

He nods and takes the box before handing me my receipt to sign. I try to rationalize my purchase with the fact that there is virtually no snow on the ground in DC—the storm that socked the area near Schuyler House went well north of DC—and it will be nice to trade my big Sorel snow boots for some sneakers. Plus, who knows? Maybe my new sneakers will motivate me to go for a much-needed run. I sign the receipt and head back outside.

It's now almost two o'clock and my stomach is growling even though it's only been a few hours since I had the bagel breakfast sandwich at the airport. Adams Morgan is known for its diversity of ethnic restaurants, and I pop into a Middle Eastern deli near the running store and order a Falafel wrap and a Coke before continuing to Logan Circle to meet Bettie, my Airbnb host. I arrive at the address that Bettie gave me a little before three o'clock, and there's a petite woman, with jet-black hair, multiple piercings and Goth-like attire pacing out front. She isn't exactly the image I had conjured up for a woman named Bettie, but I walk up to her anyway.

"Bettie?" I ask.

"Oh, hi! Yes, I'm Bettie. You must be Sarah?"

I almost correct her but then remember I booked the apartment under Sarah's name. I say a quick prayer that she doesn't notice that I don't look anything like the picture on Sarah's license as I extend my hand. "Yep, that's me. Nice to meet you!"

She opens the door to the building and motions for me to enter. She nods a hello to the doorman/security guy, and we head up to her apartment in the elevator. The apartment is on the fifth floor of what I guess is a six-story building. The urban myth in DC is that no building can be higher than the Capitol dome, but a planner for the city once told me that was completely untrue. Either way, there are no tall buildings in DC, and that, in my opinion, is one of the many things that makes the city so livable and charming.

Bettie unlocks the door to apartment 511, and I walk in to take a quick look around. It looks very much like the pictures I saw on the Airbnb website—it's a very open loft-like space with high, exposed cement ceilings and a wall of floor-to-ceiling windows. The apartment is somewhat sparsely furnished with a couch, coffee table, and TV in the living area, and I can see the foot of a bed through the bedroom door, but it appears to have all the basics and is incredibly tidy. I notice there is no dinner table but the kitchen has a nice, big island with four barstools so that should more than suffice.

Bettie walks around the island and opens and closes a few cupboards to show me that the shelves are full of glasses, plates, bowls and pots and pans. "As you can see, the place has all the kitchen stuff you need," she says as she sets the apartment keys on the kitchen island. She points out the location of the washer/dryer and gives me a piece of paper with instructions on how to use the Wi-Fi and TV before heading toward the door. "Well, that's about it. My cell number is on that piece of paper so call me with any questions. Enjoy your stay." She heads out the door, leaving me alone in the apartment.

I take a quick walk around the apartment, open and close the fridge and check the cabinets in the bathroom. The fridge is pretty bare, but there's what I estimate to be a year's supply of toilet paper and paper towels in the linen closet in the bathroom. I am utterly exhausted but feel like I should make a quick run to the store before I crash. There's a Whole Foods a few blocks away on P Street, so I pull everything out of my daypack and dump it on the couch and then head out the door with my empty pack—I know it's a cardinal sin not to bring your own bags to Whole Foods. They say there's a thing called the Whole Foods Effect since the grocery chain has a knack for opening in "up and coming" neighborhoods, and as soon as they do, real estate prices seem to skyrocket literally overnight. The Whole Foods in Logan Circle opened in 2000 when the neighborhood was definitely still considered "on the fringe." Today, only fifteen years later, the neighborhood is teeming with yuppies (gay and straight), there are hip restaurants and bars on every corner and two-bedroom condos can sell for a million dollars.

I walk the short distance to Whole Foods and grab a small cart at the entrance of the store. The place is totally mobbed, and I maneuver slowly through the aisles somehow managing to pick up some soap, shampoo, deodorant, a comb, and a small bottle of organic laundry detergent before searching out the cheese-and-wine section of the store. I select some wickedly overpriced but delicious-sounding cheese and grab a bottle of wine that's on sale and supposedly gets ninety-two points from the Wine Enthusiast before working my way over to the prepared food section to find something for dinner.

I load up a carton with pasta and vegetables and get in the line for the express checkout, which is incredibly long but moves pretty quickly because the queue feeds no fewer than twenty express registers at the front of the store.

Once I get back to the apartment, I put away my groceries, head into the bathroom, strip down, and climb in the shower. While I'm in the shower, I make a mental note to buy a razor the next time I'm at the store. I dry off and wrap the towel around my body and run a comb through my hair. I wrap another towel around my head and then pad over to the couch where I dumped the contents of my daypack. I carry everything into the bedroom so I can lay it all out on the bed and take an inventory of what I have.

- Ski hat and gloves
- Ski parka
- Fleece pants
- Three long underwear tops, one of which is heavyweight
- Down vest
- Jog bra
- Lots of socks, ski socks, wool socks, and running socks
- Flashlight
- Six-pack of Fruit of the Loom underwear
- Pad of paper and pens
- Toiletries
- Laptop and charger
- Two pair of jeans
- Belt
- Two bras
- Two long sleeve T-shirts
- V-neck sweater
- Running shoes and Sorel boots
- Running tights

I proceed to empty the pockets of my ski coat and Sarah's fanny pack and assess their contents as well. I, of course, have a ton of cash and two credit cards—Sarah's personal credit card that I found in her fanny pack plus the business credit card for Hatshepsut Consulting I got from the safe deposit box. I dig through the kitchen drawers to find some scissors and cut up Sarah's personal card and toss it in the trash.

I also have two phones—my new iPhone and the Motorola cell phone that I bought on Christmas Day in New York. I take the Motorola phone out to the kitchen and plug it into the wall and set it on the kitchen counter so it will always be visible and fully charged. The Motorola still has the SIM card associated with the "Ellen number" so I plan to keep it turned on all day, every day until I hear from Ellen.

I cut the tags off the rest of my new clothes and throw them in the washer. I add some detergent and start a load before realizing I'm wearing nothing but a towel—everything else is in the washer. I remember seeing a neatly folded bathrobe in the linen closet so, hoping it's clean, I slip it on and hang the towels back up on a hook in the bathroom.

I walk back out to the kitchen, pour myself a glass of wine, cut up some cheese, plop down on one of the kitchen stools and open my laptop. As always, I scan the main news sites. When I don't see anything new, I navigate to the website for Carbonite—a company that backs up people's personal files and saves them in the cloud so that they're protected and can be accessed from anywhere where there's a decent Internet connection. I set up a Carbonite account a few years ago mostly to make sure I never lost the important documents and all the photos on my home computer.

I log in to my Carbonite account and scan through all the files that reside on my desktop in Vermont just to make sure everything looks okay. I figure the chances that the police have found my desktop are slim because, before the incident at Schuyler House, I'd been living temporarily in an apartment in Burlington I was subletting from a rich University of Vermont graduate student. He'd decided to take time off from school to travel the world. We only had a verbal agreement; it wasn't an official lease, and I doubt that his landlord knew he had sublet the place out to me. I think his parents were paying the rent, and I don't think they even know he decided to skip town.

I was living in the apartment because I'd recently bought about twenty acres of land with only a small rustic cabin on it. I usually refer to the land as "my farm," but I don't have any animals or anything, at least not yet, so it's a stretch to call it a farm. I lived in the cabin through the summer, but it's not winterized so I'd sublet the apartment in downtown Burlington for the winter. Not long after I bought the property, I'd hired an architect to help me design my dream house to build on the land and I'd been talking to a couple of builders with hopes of breaking ground in the spring. Although now, I admit, that all seems like a distant pipe dream.

At any rate, the desktop was one of the few personal items I'd moved to the apartment with me. I figure, at this stage, the police might know about my land and the cabin but they probably don't know about the sublet. To be honest, though, my sense is that the police are looking for me but they haven't exactly launched a nationwide manhunt. I just don't sense from the news that the cops are expending major resources to hunt Ellen and me down. We didn't actually steal anything from Schuyler House, although they probably know that's what we were trying to do. And the news reports all seem to indicate that Kat and Sarah's deaths were the result of the deck collapsing rather than any foul play. Plus, the security guard is expected to make a full recovery from the injuries he sustained on Christmas Eve.

Even though they've uncovered enough information to link Ellen, Kat, Sarah, and me, I still haven't seen any indication at all that they've connected the four of us to any of the previous thefts in which we did successfully steal art. Even if the police have Sarah's computer, which they probably do, I think they're unlikely to find anything on it. We were so incredibly careful about our electronic trail when planning our burglaries, and we weren't dumb enough to deposit large amounts of cash into our personal bank accounts or buy extravagant cars that, from the outside view, were way beyond our means. Of course there's the bank account that we set up for Hatshepsut Consulting, but it would take a ton of police resources to ever link that account to any of us. As a result, I'm working really hard to convince myself that the cops will never link any of the other burglaries to us. If they did, I would likely be in a much bigger heap of trouble than I am now, assuming they're able to track me down.

Not surprisingly, this gets me wondering about the statute of limitations for our past burglaries so I Google "statute of limitations for burglary." My eyes glaze over when I start to read some of the search results. The first few sites I read are full of complicated legal definitions that spell out the difference between burglary, theft, and robbery, words that I have always used pretty interchangeably. Regardless, from what I can tell, the longest statute of limitations seems to be about five years. I decide to try a different search and instead Google "statute of limitations for Isabelle Stewart Gardner heist."

The Gardner Museum in Boston was robbed in 1990 and remains the biggest art theft (from a dollar perspective) in US history. This time the search results are more informative. I find a *New York Times* article from 2013 that says the statute of limitations for breaking into the museum has long expired, but it goes on to say that prosecutors could potentially convict someone for possession of the stolen art today. Well, the four of us were always very quick to get rid of the art we stole—we typically had it in our possession for fewer than twenty-four hours—so hopefully I'm good there.

I've been nibbling on cheese but am still pretty hungry, so I pull my pasta and vegetables out of the fridge and toss them in the microwave. I find some paper napkins and utensils in one of the kitchen drawers and sit back down at the kitchen island to inhale my food while scanning the CNN website to learn more about the blizzard in the Midwest.

After I finish eating, I move my clothes from the washer to the dryer and my mind wanders to Kat's husband Todd. Since I still haven't heard from Ellen, I decide to give him a call. First, I want to tell him how sorry I am about Kat and about everything and see how he's holding up under the circumstances. It's a good bet that the cops are putting a lot of pressure on him which seriously sucks because he just lost his wife and, although he knew what we were up to, he had no direct involvement whatsoever in any of our illicit activities. I pour myself another glass of wine, pick up my new iPhone and dial Kat's home number. It rings multiple times, and I'm about to hang up when I hear Todd's voice.

"Hello?" he says softly.

"Todd…it's me…Mattie," I say just as softly.

"Oh my God…Mattie, is that really you?" His voice trails off, and I can tell he's fighting off tears when he finally continues. "It's so good to hear your voice."

Tears well up in my eyes. "I'm so sorry about Kat. We never thought something like this would happen…How are you holding up?"

"I'm in complete and utter shock. I cannot even put into words what I am feeling right now. I can't believe she's gone." He succumbs to the tears he was trying to hold back.

He asks me what happened, and I walk him through the events at Schuyler House on Christmas Eve and everything that's happened to me since. When I'm done, I ask him, "How could we have been so stupid?" It's a rhetorical question, and he doesn't answer. "God, we should have at least had the sense to quit while we were ahead. I will never ever steal another piece of art in my life. I know that this comes a little late for Kat…and for you, but still…"

"I blame myself too," Todd says. "I should have put a stop to it a long time ago."

"Like Kat would have listened," I say with a laugh. "You know she wasn't one to take orders!"

Todd laughs. "Yeah, no one would ever describe her as being meek!"

"I'm sorry you're left to deal with the mess we created. Are the cops putting a lot of pressure on you?"

"Nah, they haven't been too bad," he says somewhat unconvincingly.

"Are you sure they haven't been too hard on you? I mean, you just lost your wife, for God's sake."

He assures me again that the police haven't been hounding him, so I move on to my next question. "Have you heard from Ellen?"

"Nope, I haven't heard anything from Ellen, but I did hear that Jake's got the boys and they're holding up all right, under the circumstances."

We chat for a little longer. I don't tell him exactly where I am now, and he doesn't ask.

Before we hang up, he tells me he's in the process of trying to schedule a memorial service for Kat and that friends and neighbors have been really supportive even given the circumstances of her death. I find a tiny bit of solace in that, give him my new Gmail address, and promise to call again soon.

CHAPTER TWELVE

I jog down P Street toward DuPont Circle and drop into the park just before officially crossing over into Georgetown. It's in the low forties outside, which isn't too bad for January, so when I woke this morning I decided to go for a run in Rock Creek Park. Once I'm in the park, I head north on the bike path toward the zoo, a path I've run hundreds of times. It feels so good to breathe in the fresh air and relieve some of the stress and sadness that I've got bottled up inside me. It doesn't take long, however, before tears begin to roll down my cheeks. I pick up my pace, but this only seems to cause the flow of tears to increase. The crying causes my nose to run, and my face quickly becomes a mess of tears and snot. *Nice.*

When I reach the zoo, I slip inside the gates and duck into the closest women's room. The zoo is a Smithsonian Institution, and, like all Smithsonian Institutions, entrance is always free of charge. Given that it's winter, the zoo, including the ladies' room, is a total ghost town. I step into one of the many empty stalls, pee and blow my nose and then step up to the bank of sinks, where I splash warm water on my face in an effort to rub away the tears on my cheeks. I glance in the mirror and, after a few more splashes of water, deem my face marginally presentable, so I head back outside.

I stretch my incredibly tight leg muscles before continuing to run north on the bike path for another mile or so before turning around to run back toward P Street. Despite the chill, it's really a beautiful day; unsurprisingly, there are a good number of joggers and bikers using the path. I am keeping up a pretty good pace and quickly cross under the Calvert Street Bridge and then under the Connecticut Avenue Bridge.

Suddenly, a big, burly guy on a mountain bike comes flying down the hill to my right. The bike path curves sharply at the bottom of the hill, and he cranks his handlebars to try and make the turn and almost takes out a woman in his path. She's forced to leap off the bike path to avoid being plowed down and tumbles down the adjacent steep grassy slope.

The biker is totally oblivious to what has happened and just continues speeding down the bike path without even a backward glance. I run ahead and hobble down the embankment to help the woman. "Are you okay?" I gasp.

"Yeah, I don't think I broke anything. I am just going to be really, really sore tomorrow morning," she pants, but manages a smile.

I offer her a hand up. Once she's on her feet, I can't help but notice that she's extremely attractive. She's about my height, slim but obviously in really good shape and she has the most incredible dark green eyes. Her light brown hair is pulled back in a ponytail, and even under her running jacket, I can tell her arms are totally buff. I stare at her a little too long but eventually find my voice. "Um, hi, I'm Mattie. What a total asshole, huh?"

"Yeah, major asshole…I'm Alex, thanks for the hand." She makes an effort to brush the dirt and grass off her running pants.

"Not a problem. Do you think you can make it home on foot or do you want me to find you a cab or something?"

"I think I am all right, but thanks. I'm not too far from home, and I think I can walk it. Thanks again, enjoy the rest of this beautiful day."

"You too." I turn to continue running back toward P Street.

I exit the park at the same place where I entered and keep running until I reach DuPont Circle. I take a few minutes to catch my breath and walk a few blocks until I reach a small corner market where I order a bagel breakfast sandwich and coffee to go, as well as pick up a bottle of orange Gatorade and a copy of the *Washington Post*.

As soon as I walk in the door to my Airbnb apartment in Logan Circle, I toss the bagel and paper on the kitchen island, guzzle some Gatorade and head into the bathroom to take a quick shower. Once I'm clean, I slip on the robe, wrap a towel around my head and walk back out to the kitchen. I wolf down my breakfast sandwich in about three bites and then nestle into the couch to nurse my coffee and scan the newspaper.

Before long, I find myself staring into space trying to figure out my next move. I've got this Airbnb apartment for the week, and then what? After my conversation with Todd last night, I desperately want to try to get to Vermont, but I know that visit's going to have to wait. I ponder my options, and staying in DC sticks out as the most logical choice. I like DC, I know DC, and I'm in DC so it makes sense for me to stay, at least for a while. When I can't think of a better plan, I commit to staying put in DC until I can figure out something better.

Now I just need to figure out where I'm going to live. Airbnb is great for the short term, but I need to find a place where I can hole up for at least a few months. I start to scan Craigslist and a couple of other apartment sites for a short-term apartment in DC. There are just a handful of listings in Logan Circle, where I would prefer to be, but the asking rents are crazy high. It's amazing how much the neighborhood has changed since I first lived here nearly a decade ago. Even under the supposed Whole Foods effect, I can't believe how quickly it has gone from a "fringe" neighborhood to the "It" neighborhood.

I expand my search radius a little to include a few additional neighborhoods and hone in on a somewhat reasonably priced partially furnished one-bedroom apartment. It's located on the border between DuPont Circle and Georgetown, which is a great location and only about a ten-minute walk from my current Airbnb apartment. I send a quick text message to the number listed for the apartment.

I close my laptop and sigh as I start to think about my personal life in Vermont. Or maybe lack of personal life is more apt. My last girlfriend and I broke up almost six months ago, and sadly, I have exactly zero prospects. Although, given my current predicament, that may not be a bad thing! It's odd, though, because I tend to be the kind of person that doesn't go for long periods of being single. As I think back, I've almost always had girlfriend, and I sure have had a lot of them over the years. Some of my relationships were really quite good and even lasted a few years, but I still haven't found that special someone. I'm a hopeless romantic, and I refuse to give up hope.

On a more pragmatic front, I consider that it's probably a damn good thing that I haven't yet broken ground on the house that I am—or was—hoping to build on my farm. However, I do have to figure out how to deal with my forensic accounting practice in Burlington. I'm a partner in a small firm, and I thank my lucky stars that the firm doesn't do any tax accounting because, if it did, the next four months would be serious crunch time. There's no "season" for forensic accounting; the work flows in steadily all year long.

Conrad Wilson is the managing partner of the firm. He's a brilliant accountant, but he's also one of the most arrogant people that I've ever met. We work extremely well together, but I wouldn't say we are friends. Still, I feel like I at least owe him the courtesy of telling him I will not be at work for the foreseeable future. He's always been decent to me and treated me with respect. It is pretty likely that he's heard about my current predicament, but I decide to give him a call anyway.

He picks up after the first ring. "Hello?" he says, his deep voice echoing in my ear.

"Conrad, it's Mattie," I reply tentatively.

"You goddam idiot," he barks.

I'm a little shaken by his tone, but I continue. "So, I take it you've heard about my, um, situation?"

"You could say that. Got a little visit from the police yesterday. Do you have any fucking idea how poorly this reflects on the firm?"

"I'm sorry, Conrad," I say weakly.

"Do you know the mess you've created? Go to hell, Mattie!" he yells, and promptly ends the call.

Well, that went well, I think to myself and lay my head against the back of the couch. I feel a migraine coming on. I pinch the bridge of my nose and close my eyes and try to clear my mind. I take a series of deep breaths to try and calm myself. The sun is still beaming in through the windows, and eventually I doze off like a cat. The chirp of an incoming text wakes me about thirty minutes later. I wipe the drool from my chin and groggily reach for my new iPhone.

Hi. Apt will be available Jan 15th. Would be happy to show you the place. Does tomorrow 9am work? It is at the corner of Q and 27th. I'll be out front. My name is Michelle.

Michelle must be the woman listing the apartment on Craigslist. I sit up and read her text again. January 15th is not ideal since I only have my current Airbnb until January 2nd, but it's unreasonable to think apartments will be ready for immediate occupancy given the tight rental market. The place looked cute online so I figure I might as well take a look at it. I text her back: *Hi Michelle. Super! I will be there tomorrow at 9am! BTW, my name is Mattie.*

I drink wine, nibble on some cheese and crackers, and scan the Internet while I wait for an order of Chinese takeout to arrive. Less than thirty minutes later, my phone buzzes. It's the doorman letting me know my food has arrived, and I tell him it's okay to let the delivery person up. I love GrubHub because no cash has to change hands—I prepay online, including the tip, and the delivery person just hands off the food. Once I have my food, I break open the containers and plop down on the couch to do some serious channel surfing. Eventually I come across an old movie called *Best in Show* on TNT and settle on that. It's a mocumentary about a dog show. I'd forgotten how incredibly funny the movie is, and I actually laugh for the first time since the Schuyler House.

CHAPTER THIRTEEN

I sleep like a rock, and I'm surprised when I wake up the next morning and it's almost eight o'clock. *Crap*! I mutter to myself. I am supposed to meet Michelle at the Q Street apartment at nine, and it will take me at least twenty minutes to walk there if I do a serious power walk. I roll out of bed, brush my teeth, jump in the shower and somehow manage to get out the door a little after eight thirty. I hightail it over to Georgetown and am only slightly sweaty and out of breath by the time I reach the corner of Q and 27th. I verify the address of the three-story U-shaped red-brick building in front of me before starting up the walk.

There's a brawny woman with shoulder-length black hair standing out front, and she extends her hand as I approach. "Hey, I'm Michelle. Let me guess, your Mattie?"

"Yep, nice to meet you Michelle." I reach out to shake her hand.

She uses a key fob to open the front door and gestures for me to enter. "After you."

I step into the small but tastefully decorated lobby. The left side is lined with what I guess is about twenty mailboxes and a row of shelves for packages and newspapers. Off to the right there's a small seating area and a storage area for bikes. Michelle follows me into the building and points me toward the staircase directly in front of us. "No elevator, it's a third-floor walk-up… Hope that's okay? You look pretty able bodied."

I nod in response, not sure if she is making a general comment or giving me a compliment.

As we walk up the stairs, Michelle explains that she and her partner Stacey are moving to Philadelphia so Michelle can start medical school and Stacey can start a new job at the Legal Aid Society. My gaydar had pretty much gone on full alert when I first saw Michelle standing outside the building, so I'm not at all surprised when she refers to her partner. She goes on to tell me that they want to rent rather than sell their condo in DC because they think it will continue to appreciate.

Once we reach the top floor, Michelle leads me to the end of the hall and unlocks the door to their condo. The unit is small, but it has a nice open kitchen and the morning sun is shining in through the living room windows. Michelle and Stacey have moved out most of their belongings except a double bed, a couch, a coffee table, a few lamps, and two kitchen barstools that will stay with the apartment. Painting supplies are piled in the corner of the living room, and there are drop cloths all over the old hardwood floors.

Michelle waves to encompass the expanse of the apartment. "Sorry for the mess. We're trying to paint the place. The walls need some patching, and it's been pretty slow going. That's why I listed the place as available January fifteenth even though we've pretty much moved out. Oh, and we're awaiting the delivery of a new washer and dryer. The old dryer conked out three days ago, and we figured we might as well replace the washer too since it was pretty much on its last leg anyway," she says with a chuckle.

I walk through the rest of the apartment and make a deliberate remark about my (nonexistent) girlfriend so that

Michelle knows for sure that I'm "family"—I figure it can only help my case as a rental candidate. The bedroom is a decent size with two large closets with mirrored folding doors. There's a slightly dated but clean full bath with a tub off the living room.

When I'm done looking around, I go back out to the living room and Michelle asks me a few personal questions like what I do for a living and if I'm from the DC area. All very reasonable questions that I try to answer as truthfully as I can without revealing too much. Generally, she seems a little giddy about renting the place to another lesbian, so I'm glad I've got that going for me.

"So, what do you think of the place?" she asks finally.

"I really like it. Any chance you would consider a nine-month lease?"

"Well, we'd really like a twelve-month lease…but I'm pretty sure that Stacey would be all right with nine months. Of course, we just need to do a credit check. I am sure you are totally solid, but Stacey only agreed to rent the place if I promised to do a credit check."

Shit, I think to myself as I smile at Michelle and try to think quickly. Naturally, any sane landlord would want to do a credit check on a prospective tenant. How did that not occur to me? "Any chance you'd be willing to skip the credit check if I pay cash for the full nine months up front?" I ask hopefully before going on to try and explain why. "It's just that my bank was hacked a few months ago and they strongly encouraged customers to freeze their credit so I did. I mean, I can "thaw" it, or whatever, but it would be sort of a hassle and I have the cash to pay in full so that just seems easier."

Michelle seems a bit taken back by my request. "Wow, I don't know," she says. "I guess it never occurred to me that someone would offer to pay up front like that. Let me, um, give Stacey a quick call and see if she's comfortable with that. Regardless, we still need you to fill out a basic rental form. It just asks for some basic personal information."

"Sure, of course," I say. "I'd be willing to finish up the painting too if it means I could move in a few days earlier," I add as she steps out into the hall to call Stacey.

I check out the kitchen a bit more closely while she's on the phone. There is ample counter space and a microwave plus a toaster and a coffeemaker on the counter. I open a couple of cupboards, and they're totally bare so I make a mental note that I need to buy silverware, plates, cups, and other kitchen stuff.

Michelle steps back into the apartment a few moments later. "Stacey's on board if you pay upfront for nine months, and we can probably be totally cleared out of here in a couple of days if you really are willing to finish up whatever painting we don't get to." I smile and she continues, "I can email you the lease later today, and you can e-sign it and send it back. If everything in the lease looks acceptable to you, it's easiest if you send us the rent money online via ZipPay. Have you used it before?"

"Yeah, I'm familiar with it," I respond.

"Okay, cool. Our ZipPay account is linked to my cell number. You have that, right?"

"Yep."

As we walk back outside, I can't help but notice that Michelle seems pretty excited about getting nine months' rent in a lump sum. We say our farewells on the sidewalk, and I walk back toward Logan Circle. I admit that I am a little giddy too, but for a different reason than Michelle. I'm psyched to have actually secured an apartment without too much incident.

I get an email from Michelle not long after I get home asking for my legal name so that she can fill in the lease. She never asked to see my ID and, since they aren't doing a credit check, they shouldn't need my social security number or anything so I figure I can take a little leeway with my legal name. She already knows that my nickname is Mattie, which, in my case is short for Matilda, but it's also is a common nickname for Martha. My last name is Pearson but people often get it wrong when they hear me say it and think my last name is Parson. So, I reply back and give her the name Martha Parson, which clearly is not my legal name but is pretty close.

Michelle shoots me the completed lease less than five minutes later, and I quickly read it over. The lease specifies January 15 as the start date, but Michelle indicates in her email that I can move in as early as the fifth if I want to. Her email also includes instructions for setting up ZipPay for the rent payment. I e-sign the lease and email it back to her and then go to the ZipPay website to send her the lump sum for nine months of rent. The money will have to come from the Hatshepsut checking account since I don't really have another option. I will just have to reimburse the checking account later—I consider the money in that account to be joint, and I don't feel right spending it, at least not until I can talk to Ellen.

Once that's done, I turn my attention to figuring out where I am going to live until I can move into Michelle and Stacey's place on the fifth. I've got my current Airbnb until January 2, but I'm hopeful that maybe I can extend my stay at the current place until the fifth or maybe even the sixth to give myself a little buffer. I log in to Airbnb's website to check the availability for my current place and it shows available all the way until the tenth of January so I submit a request to Bettie asking to extend my stay for a few more days.

I order Mexican from a place around the corner from my apartment and spend the evening binge watching episodes of *Property Brothers* on HGTV before eventually falling asleep on the couch. As a result, I wake up Monday morning with a bit of a stiff back. Even so, I still drag myself out for a run. Afterward, I stop by Starbucks for a vanilla latte and a spinach feta wrap. While I wait in line, I pick up a copy of the *New York Times* and skim the headlines. There's a big photo on the front page of workers preparing for the massive New Year's Eve crowds expected in Times Square this evening.

Wow, it hadn't even occurred to me that it was New Year's Eve. That means that nearly a week has passed since the Schuyler House… It seems like only yesterday that Kat, Sarah, Ellen, and I were making the final preparations for the Schuyler House…that Kat and Sarah were alive. My emotions are still so incredibly raw; I'm certainly not in a celebratory mood. There will be no champagne toast for me this year.

Later that afternoon, I run back over to Whole Foods to grab some wine, cheese and few frozen burritos to sustain me for the evening. I have a few glasses of wine and I'm feeling extremely melancholy by the time the big ball drops in Times Square. After that, I sit by the window and watch the street fill with people as they wander—or, in many cases, stumble—home from bars and parties. My life right now feels so unreal; it feels like I'm watching a movie.

CHAPTER FOURTEEN

A few days later, I swing by Kramer's Books—a total institution in DuPont Circle—to search for a new book to read. I am perusing the shelf with all of the *New York Times* best sellers on it when I bump into the woman that I helped in the park a few days earlier.

"Hey, it's Mattie, right? I'm Alex. You helped me in the park the other day."

"Oh, hi, yes, I remember." Like I would forget those eyes, I think to myself. "Good to see you again. How are you holding up?"

"Good as new! I think I got lucky, I didn't really do any damage to my body. In fact, was out running the next day."

"Wow, you are a real trouper!" I reply. "If it had been me, I probably would have used it as an excuse to take a few days off!"

Alex chuckles and points toward the back of the bookstore where there is a small bar. "Can I buy you a beer to thank you for coming to my rescue?"

I assure her that I was happy to help but agree, probably too eagerly, to join her for a beer.

We chat as we sip on our beers, and I learn that Alex lives in Logan Circle and is a widow.

"My husband Robert was an avid road bike rider and died about nine months ago when he was hit by a car during a ride with a few buddies on the back roads in northern Virginia," she explains.

"Wow, that's horrible. I'm sorry," I reply.

"Yeah, it's been really tough but I'm hanging in there. I know he would have wanted me to live life to the fullest and that's what I'm trying to do. He and I ran a landscaping company together, and I've been trying to keep the business afloat ever since he died."

I'm seriously impressed with Alex's tenacity. "That's incredible. Good for you," I respond.

We order a second beer, and then Alex turns to me. "So, what about you?"

"Well, let's see. There isn't much to tell. I'm an accountant—a forensic accountant, to be more precise." I play with the corners of the cocktail napkin under my beer and try not to think about Conrad, the bastard.

"What exactly is forensic accounting?" Alex asks.

"It's kind of like putting together the pieces of a financial puzzle. We comb over financial information to investigate stuff like fraud, embezzlement, money laundering, and insider trading. We typically get hired by lawyers, and sometimes law enforcement, to investigate financial records and sometimes have to testify as expert witnesses."

"Wow, that actually sounds kind of interesting."

"I think it is, but most people's eyes roll into the back of their head as soon as they hear the word accountant," I say with a laugh.

"Do you work for a firm here in DC?"

"Well, it's kind of a long story...I'm actually a partner in a firm up in Vermont, but I am, um...currently taking a little sabbatical to try my hand at writing. I used to live in DC, and it seemed like a good place to come for a little change of scene." I know I'm seriously stretching the truth when I tell her this, especially given my recent conversation with Conrad, although I've always dreamed about writing a novel.

"Wow, cool, that's brave of you! What are you writing?"

"Fiction, a novel. I've been composing it in my head for years, and I finally decided to try and put it to paper."

"Good for you! Is your, uh, family supportive?"

"Well, I'm newly single which is part of the reason why I decided that there is no time like the present. I mean, I wasn't married or anything, I just got out of a long-term relationship."

"Oh, I'm sorry."

"Nah. It's okay. It was for the best. She, my ex…" Alex raises an eyebrow when I say 'she.' "Oh, I'm gay," I blurt out. "Anyway, she and I had sort of drifted apart, if you know what I mean."

"Well, breakups are never easy no matter the circumstances. But I think it's great that you are taking this opportunity to chase one of your dreams. And lucky for me! If you hadn't, I never would have met you."

Alex's phone buzzes, and she pulls it out to see who it is. "Oh, shoot, I'm late. I am so sorry, but I've got to run." She downs the last of her beer. She slides off her barstool, throws some money on the bar, and slips on her coat.

I make a totally lame joke about people running for the hills as soon as they hear the word accountant, and she chuckles and leans in to give me a hug goodbye. She turns to leave but then stops and turns back toward me.

"Hey, I've been looking for a new running partner ever since my neighbor Patty moved to LA. Wanna try and run together sometime soon?"

"Sure, that would be awesome," I reply enthusiastically. We agree to meet at the P Street Bridge this coming Saturday.

I wander back into the bookstore section of Kramer's after Alex leaves and buy a book that I'd been eyeing before I ran into her. As I walk home, my mind quickly drifts back to Alex. She is even more attractive than I remembered, and I can't deny that I'm a little disappointed that she's straight. Oh well. I try to console myself that it will be nice to have someone to run with… I have been a little lonely since I got to DC.

* * *

I spend the next few days exploring DC like a tourist. I wander through the FDR Memorial, visit the Botanical Gardens and gawk at the Constitution, Bill of Rights, and the Declaration of Independence on display at the National Archives. On two occasions, I also slip into a nearby public library to try to call Ellen on Skype again. I have avoided calling her on my new iPhone in an effort to stay under the police's radar. I can't understand why she hasn't called me back. Something must be wrong… I'm dying to talk to her.

CHAPTER FIFTEEN

Finally, Saturday rolls around. As we discussed at Kramer's, I meet Alex at the P Street entrance to Rock Creek Park for a run. She's stretching her long, muscular legs when I walk up, and her snug running top makes it impossible not to notice her ample breasts. Damn, she's hot. She stops stretching when she notices me approaching and greets me with a giant grin. "Hey, Mattie, good to see you!"

"Hi!" is all that I manage to utter while I work to get my libido under control.

"I'm done stretching, so I'm ready whenever you are."

"I'm ready as I'll ever be. How far do you usually run?" I ask as I do a little stretching of my own.

"Usually five miles or so. What about you?"

"Five sounds good to me."

I let Alex set the pace and am pleased to discover that it's very close to my usual eight-minute mile stride. In truth, I'm sort of relieved. Alex doesn't have an ounce of fat on her, and I'd been worried she would totally leave me in the dust.

"Too bad our kamikaze friend isn't out today," Alex jokes as we run by the spot where the crazy biker almost took her out.

"Ha, ha. I can't believe you're not angry about that," I reply.

"Life's too short to let something like that get to you," Alex says.

"I like your attitude," I say.

Alex shrugs like it's no big deal. "Did you end up buying anything at Kramer's the other day?" she asks.

"Yeah, actually I did. I bought this book about a woman who decides to skip college and sail around the world by herself. So far it's fascinating."

"Wow, that's awesome. I like to think I could do something like that."

"Not me. I'm way too chicken to do something like that," I say with a laugh before asking, "What about you, did you pick up anything at Kramer's?"

"Yeah, I bought that book *A Walk in the Woods* by Bill Bryson. I've been meaning to read it forever. I love any book about the outdoors and I've always liked his sense of humor."

"Oh yeah, I always wanted to read that too but never got around to it," I reply.

"Well, I'd be happy to give it to you when I'm done,"

"That would be great, thanks. And, if you want, I can give you my book about the sailing woman,"

"Cool, we can form our own mini book club!" Alex says with a laugh.

"What a great idea! I absolutely love to read."

"Me too," Alex says and gives me a wink.

We chat easily for the rest of the run. Before I know it, we're back to P Street. We walk back to DuPont Circle and part ways, but not before agreeing to run together again a few days later.

* * *

After our run, I head back to my Airbnb apartment and take a quick shower before packing up my limited belongings. I jam my computer and clothes into my backpack, zip all my cash securely into the pockets of my ski coat and then carefully place the Motorola phone and my iPhone into Sarah's fanny pack. I take one more look around the apartment to make sure I've got everything, hoist my backpack onto my back and head out to meet Michelle. I'm meeting her to get the keys to my new apartment. I'm excited; there's a skip to my step as I head toward Georgetown. Just like before, Michelle is standing out on the front walk waiting for me when I arrive even though I'm a few minutes early. She greets me with a broad smile.

As we walk in the building, she hands me a Yoda keychain with two keys and a fob. "The fob is for the front door, the small key is for the mailbox and the other key opens both locks on the apartment door," she explains.

We head up the stairs to the apartment, and she rattles off some basic instructions like who to call if I get locked out and what to do with my garbage. Per the lease, they've left the cable and Internet service on because it's included in the rent, and Michelle shows me how to use the remote and hands me a piece of paper with the Wi-Fi name and password. Then she turns to leave. "Well, I better get going. Stacey will be pulling up out front any moment. We're headed straight to Philly to get settled in our new place. Call or text me if you need anything."

Once she's gone, I pull off my coat and start to make a list of stuff I need to buy. I already know I need silverware, plates, and cups, but I jot down a bunch of other stuff too: wine opener, cutting board, salt and pepper, wineglasses, napkins… The list quickly becomes long, and I haven't even considered food yet.

After the kitchen, I move on to do an inventory of the bathroom and peek under the sink and in the linen closet to find a few rolls of toilet paper but not much else. I add sheets, towels, Formula 409, sponges, and soap to my list before pausing to look above the washer/dryer combo for laundry detergent. Negative, so I add that and dryer sheets to my list too. There is a Target in Columbia Heights, not too far from my apartment, so I figure I can get most of the household stuff on my list from there. I'll worry about groceries later. There's a big Safeway grocery store in Georgetown—dubbed the Social Safeway (or sometimes the

Singles Safeway) by local residents because of its reputation as a place where Georgetown's singles meet and exchange glances while cruising the aisles—so I can swing by there when I get back from Target.

I will either have to walk or take a taxi to Target since there is no Metro stop that is convenient to Georgetown. The myth is that the wealthy Georgetown residents blocked a station from being built to help keep the riffraff out of the neighborhood, but in reality, building a station in Georgetown would have been prohibitively expensive. As a result, it was never seriously considered. Not to say that the residents would not have blocked it if one had been proposed.

I pull on my coat and decide to quickly check Google Maps for the exact address of Target. I reach down to pull my iPhone out of the fanny pack but the fanny pack isn't there. My mind starts racing. The Motorola phone is in the fanny pack too. I remember putting the phones in the fanny pack before I left the Airbnb, but I don't recall actually clipping it around my waist.

"Shit," I mutter. I must have left it on the kitchen counter. Luckily, I've got the Airbnb place for one more day. I'm not scheduled to give Bettie back the keys until tomorrow morning. I'll just to have to go back and get the fanny pack when I'm done shopping.

CHAPTER SIXTEEN

I wander back to the apartment in Logan Circle to get the fanny pack later that afternoon. I take the elevator up to the fifth floor and see them a second too late. Two uniformed police officers are standing in front of the door to apartment 511, and they spot me just as I'm stepping off the elevator.

I hear the elevator doors close behind me, and my heart starts racing like mad. There is no time to think. There are stairwells at both the north and south end of the hall, and I take off for the one at the north end. One of the cops yells something at me, and I hear them start to run down the hall in my direction. I pass a large decorative planter in the hallway and kick it. The cops easily scramble over it, but it slows them down a little bit.

I hurl myself through the fire door and run down two flights of stairs. Rather than run to ground level, I open the door on the third floor and take off toward the stairway at the south end of the building.

I no longer hear the cops behind me. By some miracle, they must not have realized that I slipped out of the stairwell on the third floor. I fly down the south stairs until I reach ground level, shove open the door and find myself in the alley behind the apartment building. I sprint toward fifteenth Street and run for three blocks before I slow to catch my breath.

Crouching behind a brick wall, I scan the street for any sign of the two cops. The coast appears to be clear. I take a deep breath and step back out to the sidewalk and try to blend in with the slew of people walking home from work.

Eventually, I make it back to my apartment in Georgetown. I flop down on the couch in the living room and cover my face with my hands and try to absorb what just happened.

"Think Mattie, think!" I say to myself. Where did I slip up? How did they find me?

It takes me about thirty seconds to come up with an answer. Conrad! That stupid fuck! He told the cops I'd called him, and they'd somehow tracked me down.

"God dammit!" I yell. I'm conscious of the fact that I also called Todd, but I know it wasn't Todd who ratted me out. Todd's like a brother to me, and I know with my whole heart that he'd never do something like that. Conrad, on the other hand…

It then occurs to me that the damn fanny pack is still inside Bettie's apartment. I curse some while I consider my options. I'm hesitant to go back to the apartment, but I've got to get that Motorola phone. It's the only connection I have to Ellen. Plus, if I can help it, I'd rather the cops not get their hands on my iPhone.

* * *

That evening, I hastily devise a plan to dress up like a maintenance man before I return to get my fanny pack. I figure pretending to be a man will help me elude the cops if they just happen to be staking out Bettie's apartment building. I go back to Target first thing the next morning and buy a Washington Redskins baseball hat, a pair of men's work pants, a pair of work boots, a gray T-shirt and pair of cheap reading glasses. I go home, put on my new clothes, tuck my hair up into the baseball hat and don my new reading glasses before heading back to Logan Circle.

It's midmorning when I round the corner onto P Street. I pause to scan the street for cops before slowly making my way to the parking garage under Bettie's building. The key fob that I have for the building should work on all its doors and entering from the parking garage seems safer than strolling by the security guard who sits at the front desk 24/7.

I am on pins and needles as I start to creep across the cavernous parking garage. It's eerily quiet. I do my best to stay in the shadows. When I'm about halfway across the garage, the door to the building opens and a man walks out. I dive behind a parked car and hide until he pulls out.

At this point, it occurs to me that there are probably security cameras in the garage. If that's the case, the front desk guard can probably see me on one of his monitors. Diving behind cars is likely to look suspicious. I'm probably better off playing it cool and sauntering into the building like I don't have a care in the world. With this in mind, I step out from behind the car and follow the well-lit walkway to the building.

With a wave of my fob, the door to the building clicks open. I step inside and quickly debate stairs or elevator. Elevator. I hit the button and wait for the car. The doors open, and two women step out. I smile at them, but they don't even look at me. I step on the elevator and press "5." The elevator starts to inch upward. I hold my breath, praying it doesn't stop at the main lobby level. The "L" lights up on the display and then the "1." I take a deep breath to try and calm my nerves. It's a lost cause.

The doors open on five, and I panic. I'm afraid to step off the elevator. It's like my feet are glued to the floor. The doors close, but the elevator doesn't move because I haven't selected a new floor.

"Get a grip," I say out loud, and then stab the "Open Door" button. I jump off the elevator as soon as the doors reopen. I remind myself of the building's security cameras and walk to door 511 like a maintenance man on a mission.

Once inside, I grab the fanny pack off the counter and toss Bettie's keys on a table near the door before I slip back out of the apartment. Hopefully, Bettie has another set of keys because I sure as hell am not meeting her back here tomorrow morning.

Quickly, I walk to the end of the hall and then run down the stairs to the alley. My heart is beating so fast that my eyeballs feel like they're pulsing. I trot down the alley and turn onto fifteenth Street, constantly looking behind me.

After three blocks, I start to calm down a little. I slow my pace as I unzip the fanny pack. I pull out my iPhone, power it down and toss it into the first garbage can I pass. It kills me to throw away a brand-new iPhone, but I am convinced that's how the cops tracked me down, and I'm certainly not going to risk it and take it to my new apartment. I have no choice but to buy a new one.

I change out of my disguise as soon as I get home and grab a beer out of the fridge even though it's only early afternoon. I sit at my kitchen island and sip my beer while I contemplate my next move. I briefly consider fleeing DC but quickly decide against it. That's what the cops will expect me to do. I convince myself that the police don't know about my new apartment. If they did, they'd have already come knocking.

CHAPTER SEVENTEEN

A couple of days later, I meet Alex again for a morning run. We meet earlier than normal; and it's still dark and cold when we set off into the park. Alex must be a morning person because she's more chatty than normal. She tells me a funny story about her crew finding a client in a compromising position the day before when they went to landscape around her pool.

"Does that kind of stuff happen a lot?" I ask.

"Let's just say that you see a lot when you spend hour upon hour working around people's homes. You're in their personal space. Some people forget that we're right outside their window and some people are well aware that we are there and just don't care what we see."

"That's crazy," I say.

"Yeah, but if you think about it, people in a lot of professions must see some wild stuff. Think about the stories that wedding planners and real estate agents could tell. I mean, the bridezilla stories have got to be abundant!"

I let out a laugh. I'm beginning to realize that Alex has a great sense of humor.

We run in silence for a while, but Alex breaks the silence when we near the final stretch. "I'm having a few friends over for dinner this Saturday. Any chance you could join us?"

"Sure, I would love to! What can I bring?"

"Great! Say seven o'clock-ish? No need to bring anything! Oh, you don't have any food allergies, do you?"

"Seven works, and nope, no food allergies. I'll eat pretty much anything."

The sun is up by the time we finish our run, but it's still really chilly, so I do a slow jog back to my apartment to stay warm. I take the stairs two at a time and practically run over Stella, the elderly woman who lives across the hall, as she's taking out her garbage. We chat briefly before I politely excuse myself so that I can go back to my apartment and take a much-needed shower. Stella is lovely and I try to help her out with chores and errands when I can but she'll talk your ear off if you let her.

My mind wanders to Alex while I'm in the shower. It occurs to me that I have absolutely nothing to wear to her house for dinner. Aside from my running outfit, I haven't bought any more clothes since my shopping spree at Macy's in New York the day after Christmas. It also occurs to me that I still only have the Fruit of the Loom flowered underwear that I picked up at Duane Reade in New York, so maybe I should get something a tad bit sexier… No surprise that thoughts of Alex makes me want to buy sexier undergarments.

I don't have any plans for the rest of the day, so I take the Metro Silver Line out to Tysons Corner, the largest and nicest shopping mall in the metropolitan area. First, I go to Saks and buy a nice pair of black jeans, a gray cashmere sweater and a pair of black leather cowboy boots. I pass the lingerie department on my way down the never-ending maze of escalators, and I relent and buy a few new pairs of underwear and a black lace bra. Next, I go to Hermes and buy a totally overpriced black leather belt and some perfume before continuing on to Macy's where I buy a few silk T-shirts to wear under my sweater. I wander through a few more stores and end up buying a sort of dressy down coat so that I can stop wearing my ski coat everywhere.

CHAPTER EIGHTEEN

Over the next few days, I wear my new cowboy boots everywhere I go in an attempt to break them in a little bit. When Saturday finally rolls around, they look a little less brand new. I slip them on and head off to Alex's place in Logan Circle. I stop into a little wine shop on my way and buy a nice bottle of red and a bottle of white to bring as a hostess gift even though Alex said not to bring anything.

Most of the buildings on her street were elaborate auto showrooms and auto repair shops in the 1930s and '40s. They were all converted into trendy lofts during the most recent real-estate boom. Her building only has about a dozen units, and it doesn't have a doorman. I locate a silver phone in the vestibule and use the arrow keys to scroll through the digital resident directory. I press the "Call" button when I come across the name Holland. Alex picks up after the first ring, tells me to come up to the fifth floor and buzzes me into the building. I take the elevator up to the top floor and am pleasantly surprised to find her standing in the open doorway to her apartment when I get off the elevator.

"Hey, Mattie. I'm so glad that you could make it!"

I give her a big smile and hand her the wine. "For you."

"I told you not to bring anything, but thank you. I will never refuse wine." She laughs and gestures me into the apartment.

I step inside and take a quick look around her place while I take off my coat. "This place is really amazing, Alex," I say as Alex hangs my coat in the front hall closet. Her loft is small and cozy but exquisitely decorated. The kitchen opens into a sunken living room filled with comfortable-looking contemporary furniture and a large, brick wood-burning fireplace. The far wall of the living room has floor-to-ceiling windows that offer great views of the city, and the rest of the walls are covered with art.

"Come on. What can I get you to drink!" Alex takes my hand and leads me into the kitchen.

"White wine would be great if you have some open."

There are two women chatting in front of the fridge, and Alex introduces us while she pours me a glass of white wine before running off to meet another arriving guest.

The woman Alex introduced as Karen turns to me. "So, how do you know Alex?" I tell them the story of the wild biker who almost took Alex out when she was running in the park. "I just happened to be running by when it happened," I explain.

"Wow, that's a crazy story. I remember Alex telling me about that kamikaze," Karen says with a chuckle.

Eventually, the conversation turns to the booming real-estate market in Logan Circle, and I learn that both women are real estate agents in the District. "I actually helped Alex buy this place a few months after Robert died," Karen explains.

"Wow, really? I love this place. Where did they live before he died?" I ask.

"They had a cute house in Takoma Park. I think Robert pushed for the house in Takoma Park so that he could have a little bit of land but Alex is more of a city girl. I think she wanted to move to a place that was more in the center of things and wasn't full of memories of Robert."

"Well she certainly has a good eye for décor and art," I reply.

"Yeah, they had a lot of this art at their house in Takoma Park but it's all Alex. She's the one that collected whenever they traveled."

* * *

Over dinner, I chat with a man named Doug who introduces himself as Karen's boyfriend, and with Alex's neighbors, Matt and Gleason, a super cute gay couple that own an architecture firm together. I have a really nice evening; I like all her friends immensely.

I don't get much time to chat with Alex until after dinner when she offers to give me a tour of her place. As we move through each room, she shares stories about various pieces of furniture. "I got this bench in Turkey," she says as we enter what she calls her study. "The cutest old man was making them, and I think of him with a smile every time I rest my feet on it." She then points out a piece that she got in South Africa and another from Vietnam.

"So, it sounds like you like to travel," I say as we move toward the master bedroom.

"Yeah, you could say that," she replies. "Robert and I used to go on a big trip every year during the off-season. It was one of the perks of running a landscaping company. We busted our asses nine months a year and then we'd go on a trip somewhere for a month or two. We always traveled on the cheap, but we went to so many amazing places and had so many wonderful experiences," she says with a little sadness in her voice.

"I am seriously jealous," I reply. "That sounds incredible."

"Yeah, but unfortunately, I wasn't able to get away this winter. I'm so overwhelmed trying to run this business by myself. This off-season, I'm just trying to play catch-up."

We turn to enter her bedroom and I can't help but smile. The space is so inviting. There is a giant floor to ceiling bookshelf packed with books. Colorful rugs dot the hardwood floor and, like the living room, the walls are covered in art. "Tell me about some of the art," I say.

"Well, I got a lot of it during our travels," she replies. "But I also picked up some of the pieces here in DC. There are a few local artists that I just love. I pop by their studios whenever they have an opening or whatever and usually end up buying something. I love the work but I also like to support the starving artists," she says with a laugh.

"I love art too," I blurt out and then quickly try and change the subject before she can ask me any art-related questions. "I love your home. It's so warm. Thank you for the tour."

* * *

As I walk back to my place after dinner, my mind immediately wanders to Alex. Tonight was the first time that I have seen her "dressed up." Her scoop-neck cashmere sweater exposed just a hint of cleavage, and her snug boy-cut jeans accentuated her totally amazing body... Get a grip, Mattie, I warn myself. I try unsuccessfully to think of something less perilous while admitting that I am totally falling for Alex no matter how hard I try to fight it.

When I get home, I slip off my coat, flip on the TV to watch *Saturday Night Live* and walk into the kitchen to pour myself a glass of sparkling water. I reach up to pull a glass from one of the kitchen cupboards and stop dead in my tracks. The light on the Motorola phone is blinking to indicate that I have a message. Slowly, I set the glass down and grab the counter to steady myself. I can't breathe. Ellen is the only one I have given this number to... I try not to get my hopes up; it's probably just a telemarketer.

I unplug the phone from the wall, sink down on one of the kitchen stools and start to listen to the message. Tears well up in my eyes the second I hear Ellen's voice. Her voice is so soft, almost a whisper.

"Hey Mat...Oh, my God...I got your note in the safe deposit box. I can't tell you how happy I was to see it. I'm in New York...There is so much we need to talk about."

She leaves a number, and I call her back right away. She picks up after the second ring.

"El?" I ask with a cry.

"Mat, is that you?"

"Yeah, it's me."

"Kat, Sarah—they're dead," she says, and immediately starts sobbing.

"I know…" The floodgates open. I start sobbing too. All the grief I've been bottling up suddenly spills out. I'm like a teapot that's reached a boil. "I tried to call you so many times," I manage finally.

"I lost my phone at Schuyler House," she explains with a sniffle.

Eventually, we make a plan to get together in New York a few days later so we can talk everything through in person.

After I hang up with Ellen, I've lost my interest in SNL, so I flip off the TV, turn out the lights and head to bed. Although my conversation with Ellen was brief, it's left me emotionally drained. Every day I've held out hope that I would hear from her…the fact that I just heard her voice is almost surreal.

CHAPTER NINETEEN

I meet Alex for a run Tuesday morning. As usual, she's stretching at our meeting spot when I arrive.

"Hey, you," she says playfully when I jog up beside her.

"Hey! Thanks for dinner on Saturday night. I really had a great time. Your friends are all super nice."

"I am really glad you could make it. How was the rest of your weekend?"

I stare back at her somewhat blankly as I flash back to my conversation with Ellen but finally find my voice. "Um, good, thanks. You?"

"Pretty mellow. I stayed up too late with Matt and Gleason Saturday night. They had some super special whiskey that they insisted I try," she says with a grin as we head down into the park. "I went for a super long run yesterday to punish myself, and I'm a little bit sore. You mind if we run a little slower today?"

"Not at all. I'm feeling a little sluggish." It's true; I haven't slept well since I spoke to Ellen. I just flop around in my bed at night like I'm a fish out of water.

I really struggle to keep up with Alex at first, and she notices. "Everything okay with you, Mattie?" She gives me a concerned look.

I'm touched that she notices I'm a little off. "Yeah, I've just got a lot on my mind." I feel guilty for giving her such a lame response, but I don't really have a choice. She's seems like a pretty open person, and I feel like I'm coming off like a cold fish. "I'm heading to New York City later today," I say enthusiastically.

"I love New York. Are you going for fun or for work?" she asks.

"For fun. I'm going to see some friends."

"Cool. Any special occasion?"

"Nah, just haven't seen them in a while and looking forward to catching up," I reply. I am tempted to tell her that I just lost two friends and that my trip is related to that, but I bite my tongue. Better to keep my past where it belongs—in the past.

The P Street Bridge appears in the distance and we slow to a walk to cool down a bit. "Have a blast in New York! Text me when you get back," Alex says before we part ways.

"Will do," I say as we wave good-bye.

I run all the way back to my apartment to take a quick shower before grabbing a cab to Union Station so that I can catch the ten o'clock Amtrak Acela to New York. The Acela is faster than the regular "Regional" Amtrak train and I should arrive in New York by midafternoon.

* * *

As soon as I get off the train in New York, I head straight for the main Amtrak lobby on the upper level of Penn Station. Ellen said she would meet me near the Eighth Street side of the station and, once I get up to the upper level, I immediately spot her tall slim figure standing on the opposite side of the lobby. I call out to her and start waving my hands like a crazy woman as I run toward her. As soon as we reach each other, she throws her arms around me and I completely fall apart. We stand in the middle of Penn Station clutching each other and sobbing into each other's shoulders. Of course, given that we are in New York City, no one even bats an eye at our teary reunion. Eventually, Ellen pulls back, wipes the tears from her face and reaches for my hand. She leads me outside so we can hail a taxi.

There is a long line of taxis at the curb outside the station, and we jump in the first one. Ellen gives the driver an address on the Upper East Side. I must have a confused look on my face because she quickly explains where we are headed. "Oh, yeah, I guess I haven't had the chance to tell you that I have my own apartment. I'll give you the full scoop later, but believe it or not, Andy and Sandy set me up with a vacant apartment in one of their buildings. In return, I offered to help them with some legal work." Andy and Sandy are our mutual friends, and they run a small but growing real estate firm in New York. They own a handful of apartment buildings. Andy manages the financing side, and Sandy oversees the legal and marketing side.

"Wow, that's awesome. They have always been the kindest people," I respond.

Ellen's apartment is a small but airy one-bedroom in a building with a doorman. She directs me to just toss my bag on the floor in the living room and then pulls me into a hug. "I can't believe you are here…after all of these weeks of wondering what happened to you." She walks over to the fridge and pulls out a couple of beers. "Hungry?"

"Famished!"

She whips a laptop out of nowhere. "Pizza?" I nod and she asks me my topping preferences before placing the delivery order online.

We grab our beers and sit down on the couch in her living area and proceed to talk for hours, interrupted only by the pizza deliveryman. We walk through everything that happened at Schuyler House on Christmas Eve and everything we've been through since that night. I tell her about the stolen truck, the Jewish skiers, and my eventual journey to DC, omitting for the time being any mention of Alex. Occasionally, she interrupts me with questions, and she remarks on my good fortune to cross paths with the Jewish skiers, but otherwise she just listens.

When I am finally finished, we get up for a quick bathroom break and then resume our positions on the couch so she can tell me her story.

She clears her throat. "Well, as you mentioned, I was inside Schuyler House when the deck collapsed…It was totally surreal," she starts. "The three of you were standing right in front of me, and then, you were just gone. All I could see beneath me were dark gray rocks surrounded by an otherwise snowy white background…I couldn't see any of you…"

Ellen takes a deep breath before continuing. "I cried out each of your names over and over again but heard only silence in return. There was no way I could climb back out the window once the deck collapsed. The area off the back of the house just dropped off down the cliff. So, I decided to take the risk and exit the house through the side door, the door we had planned to use to escape the house with the art. Of course, I knew opening this door would set off the alarm, but it seemed like maybe we had bigger problems at the moment." She's talking quickly now, and pauses briefly to collect her thoughts before continuing. "Once I finally made it outside, I was able to scramble partway down the rocky cliff and kept crying out to each of you but still heard nothing in return. I remember thinking that it was so eerily quiet. The only sound I could hear was the river running below. And then…" Ellen takes a few deep breaths.

I rub her back until she's finally able to continue. "…And then…I found Sarah," she says as she starts to sob uncontrollably. After a couple more deep breaths, she continues between sobs. "I knew right away…that she was…dead. There was so much blood. Oh, God, Mattie, it was absolutely horrible. I guess she must have hit the rocks pretty hard when the deck collapsed. I cried out to you and Kat and tried to climb farther down the cliff, but it was hopeless. It was so steep and it was dark and the snow was so deep…" I take her hand again and offer her a partially used tissue from my sleeve. She blows her nose and gets up to get us each a glass of water before sitting back down to finish her story.

"I didn't know what to do so I started to climb back up the rocks and eventually fought my way through the snow to try and find the snowmobiles. I was utterly distraught when I saw that both snowmobiles were right where we'd left them. When I found Sarah but not you and Kat, I'd prayed that you two had made it back to the snowmobiles and escaped, but when I saw that they were both there, I just assumed that meant that you and Kat had met the same fate as Sarah. I started to freak out even more. I started to dig frantically for my phone so that I could call 911, but I couldn't find it anywhere. It must have fallen out of my pocket when I was scrambling on the rocks."

She looks up at me with her bloodshot eyes and takes a few sips of water before continuing her story. "I took one of the snowmobiles and drove it back to the Tahoe. I started to load the snowmobile up on the trailer behind the Tahoe but then figured why bother. I just ditched it into a snowbank and climbed into the SUV. I just sat there like a complete zombie until I finally put the truck in gear and drove off in no particular direction. It was still snowing like mad, and it was all I could do to keep the Tahoe on the road. After driving for thirty minutes or so, I pulled over and stared at the car's navigation system to try and figure out where the hell I was. I zoomed the map in and out and tried to decide where I should go. Suddenly, I remembered the Freemonts' cabin."

Mark Freemont was a guy Ellen had dated all through high school, and his family has a cabin on Saranac Lake. Ellen probably spent half her summers up at the place. Gosh, I'd even spent a few weekends at their cabin myself when we were in high school. It was fairly isolated, but we always had so much fun waterskiing, sailing, hiking, and building big bonfires at night. "Yeah, I remember that place."

"Well, as far as I could remember, the Freemonts' place was never winterized so I felt pretty certain no one would be there in December, especially not over Christmas. They really only ever used the place in the summer and occasionally during hunting season. Given the snow on the roads, it took me forever to get there, and even with my navigation system, I was pretty amazed that I even found it.

"The door was locked but they still hide the key in the same place so I let myself in. I stayed at the cabin for almost two weeks, and at first I was sure that someone would see the smoke coming from the chimney and call the police or something, but I finally realized that I was just being overly paranoid. There were a few cans of soup and Hormel chili in the kitchen so I lived off that for a few days before I got up the nerve to drive into town and buy groceries."

She goes on to explain that the cabin has satellite TV so she was able to follow the little news there was about Schuyler House. "I remember being so confused when the newscasters first reported that two bodies were found. I was so certain that all three of you had died, and it wasn't until they identified Sarah and Kat that I began to wonder if maybe you'd gotten away somehow. The cabin doesn't have a phone and I didn't have a computer, so I started to go stir-crazy. Plus, I was anxious to figure out what had happened to you. I finally made up my mind to try to get to New York.

"I drove the Tahoe to Albany and parked it at a Dunkin' Donuts about a mile away from the Albany train station. I didn't have much in the way of belongings and I wanted to conserve the limited amount of cash I had on me, so I just walked the mile to the train station. I bought a ticket on the next Amtrak train to Penn Station, and once I got to New York, I literally just showed up on Andy and Sandy's doorstep. They were a little surprised to see me, to put it mildly!"

We both laugh before she continues. "After I was in New York for a week or so, I decided to visit the bank safe deposit box. That's when I saw my note and called you."

"God, I'm so glad you found it! I don't know how we would have found each other otherwise."

"It was so smart of you to leave it there for me sweetie!" She reaches over and squeezes my hand affectionately.

After a few minutes of silence, I turn to Ellen. "What about your house in Stowe?"

"My brother Ethan has been keeping an eye on the place, and he gets up there most weekends when he has the kids. Plus

I told Andy and Sandy they could use it anytime they wanted," she replies as she stands up to stretch.

Stowe is an absolutely adorable town in Vermont that is home to one of the state's largest ski and golf resorts. Ellen had been living in her brother's ski house in Stowe ever since she moved back to Vermont after her divorce. Ethan got some crazy interest-only, no-money-down mortgage and bought the ski house just before the housing market imploded in 2008. In reality, he couldn't really afford the house and unsurprisingly was on the verge of losing it when Ellen moved back to Vermont. She needed a place to live and was flush with cash so she paid off the mortgage. In exchange, her brother let her live there although he technically still owned the house.

* * *

It's late by the time we finish sharing our stories, and we're both starting to yawn with some frequency. Ellen helps me make up the pull-out couch in her living room and wishes me a good night. I change into sweats and a T-shirt, brush my teeth and fall into bed. I'm out cold three seconds after my head hits the pillow and I sleep hard until almost nine o'clock the next morning.

I feel extremely groggy, but I climb out of bed and wander into Ellen's small galley kitchen in search of some strong coffee. She has one of those fancy Nespresso coffee machines, and it takes me awhile to figure out how to turn it on. I smile triumphantly when it finally starts to gurgle and secrete rich-looking coffee.

Ellen emerges from her room just as I am taking my first sip of coffee. Her normally perfectly coifed black hair looks like a hornets' nest.

"Morning! Looks like you combed your hair with an egg beater," I say with a laugh. She gives me a blank look. "My mom used to always say that about my hair when I emerged for breakfast before I got ready for school."

She gives me a crooked grin. "Believe it or not, I slept like a rock!"

"Yeah, I did too! It was seriously therapeutic to talk through all the Schuyler House stuff with you last night."

"Yeah, God, I couldn't agree more. I'm so damn glad that you are here." She gives me a quick hug and then reaches for a coffee mug. After Ellen makes her coffee, she walks over and opens her front door and grabs something off the door handle. "Ta-da! The *New York Times*," she says as she holds up the paper.

We both sit at the kitchen counter and slowly sip our coffee while we scan the paper until my growling stomach rudely interrupts us.

Ellen looks up. "Guess we should go grab something to eat, huh?"

I nod in agreement, and we each throw on some clothes and go in search of food.

"There's an old-school diner down the street," Ellen suggests.

"I think that's just what the doctor ordered!"

We totally gorge ourselves on eggs, sausage, and hash browns and then wander over toward Central Park. We stroll around the reservoir before heading back to Ellen's apartment to take a little nap.

That evening, we go out to dinner, and I catch the train back to DC the next morning.

CHAPTER TWENTY

The morning after my return to DC is gray and rainy, but Alex and I made plans to run, so I drag myself out of bed. I slip a rain jacket on over my running clothes and head out the door. Alex is waiting for me when I reach our usual meeting spot.

"So, how was your trip to New York?" she asks as soon as I'm within earshot.

I pause. "Extremely therapeutic!" I say finally, which is true; the trip was incredibly therapeutic in its own way.

Alex finishes her stretching and stands up. "Ready?"

I can't help but notice that she looks exhausted. Once we get underway, I ask her if everything is all right. She lets out an audible sigh and reluctantly admits that she's totally overwhelmed trying to keep on top of the finances for Hemlock, her landscaping company.

"I hate to admit it, but Robert mostly dealt with the financial side of things at Hemlock. I always vowed to get more involved with them, but we just never found the time…"

Without really thinking, I blurt, "I could help." Honestly, I would love to help her out, and it would give me something productive to do. I miss working with numbers.

She looks over at me with surprise. "Really? I mean, if you're serious, then that would be really awesome. Of course we have an accountant, but he mostly just deals with our taxes and the bigger stuff. Robert got us using this company called PayChex and they handle our basic payroll, so I'm good there. It's the day-to-day invoices and budgeting that has me overwhelmed… Are you sure you have the time?"

"Sure, I have some time, and yes, I'm serious. I'd be happy to help."

When we had beers at Kramer's, I'd mentioned that I was an accountant but that I was taking a sabbatical to write. I mumble something about having a bad case of writer's block and needing a diversion. I hope this sort of explains why I have some free time on my hands.

We're both eager to get out of the miserable weather when we finish our run; we quickly say our good-byes and agree to meet at her office the following Monday so I can peek at the Hemlock financials.

* * *

When Monday rolls around, I grab a late lunch and wander over to meet Alex at her office. Hemlock is located in the second story of an old stone building on Seventeenth Street in the DuPont Circle neighborhood. I skip the elevator and take the steps to the second floor, enter through a frosted-glass door that has Hemlock Landscaping stenciled on the front and smile at the woman sitting at the reception desk.

She looks up from her computer when I walk in. "Hello. May I help you?" she asks with a smile.

"Hi, yeah. I'm here to meet Alex Holland. My name is Mattie," I say as I look around the small but open office that's buzzing with activity. The place has an industrial feel with exposed brick, exposed ductwork, and big warehouse-like windows. Everyone is very casually dressed. A few people are working at standing drafting tables, but most are sitting in front of large iMac computer screens.

"Sure, let me give her a call."

Moments later, Alex pops her head out of a nearby doorway, smiles broadly in my direction and motions for me to come on back to her office. As always, just the sight of her is enough to send my stomach flip-flopping. She gives me a quick hug hello when I reach her office and leads me over to a small table near the window that is piled high with papers. "These piles are my current accounting system! I hope you know what you are getting yourself into." She laughs.

There's a wooden chair in front of the table, and Alex gestures for me to sit while she drags her desk chair over so that she can sit next to me. She tries to explain the method by which the piles on the table are "organized." Then she grabs a laptop off a nearby bookshelf, pops it open and shows me some of the reports that Robert created to keep track of invoices and expenses. Some of the reports are simple spreadsheets in Excel and others are in QuickBooks.

After she's done going over the current state of things, I look up at her with what I hope is an encouraging smile. "All right, I think I got it. Let me take a little time to weed through some of this and see what I can do to help."

She gives me a look of relief. "Have at it! I will be in the other room looking over some plans that a designer's putting together for a house in Woodley Park, but feel free to interrupt if you have any questions or need anything, okay?"

I nod and turn back toward the desk to get to work. First, I scan the various reports that Robert created and then try to weed through and organize the pile of papers on the desk. My initial assessment is that Robert did seem to have a decent, albeit very basic, system in place to track income and expenses. However, very few of the reports have been updated since he died. As a result, Alex probably doesn't have a very good handle on where the business stands financially. I figure that I should start back around the time he died and try to get everything updated in QuickBooks and Excel. Then I can start to try and analyze the figures.

I spend a few hours at it and I am deep into one of Robert's Excel spreadsheets when Alex comes back into the office to check on me. "So, it's a mess, huh?"

"I wouldn't say it's a mess. Things just need to be updated and analyzed so that we can get a good picture of your financial health," I respond.

"So you think you can do all that? I'll pay you whatever you want!" Alex almost begs.

I give her a crooked smile. "Sure, I can do all that. Like I said yesterday, I've got writer's block so I would welcome some part-time accounting work. I don't think it'll be too hard to get everything cleaned up and organized. What do you say I spend some time getting everything in order and then we can decide where to go from there?"

"Sounds like a plan! Thank you so much, Mattie. I'll have Renee, the receptionist, set up a desk and computer for you. That way you can have your own space to work."

"Okay, thanks, Alex."

"You're more than welcome to transfer Robert's files from the laptop to the desktop. I'm sure it will be much easier to work with all those numbers on a big desktop screen."

"Yeah, I think you're right."

I stand up and collect my coat and bag. Alex walks me back up to the front of the office and gives me a hug good-bye. As I walk home from Hemlock, I admit I'm actually excited to conquer the Hemlock finances. Of course, it also means that I get to spend more time with Alex, which is a major bonus, but I'm starting to get a little lonely. It will be nice to have something more to keep me occupied.

CHAPTER TWENTY-ONE

I'm able to get a handle on the Hemlock finances fairly quickly. Luckily, the numbers tell a decent story: The company is on very strong footing financially. Business has been very good, and on top of that, Alex told me they're usually able to get away with charging a bit of a premium because they've built such a strong reputation. I stretch back in my chair and hear Alex finish up a phone call in her office. I check the clock on my computer and it's almost six o'clock, so I get up and poke my head into her office.

"Knock, knock. Feel like grabbing dinner somewhere?"

She looks up at me with a weary smile. "Sure! I'm definitely ready to call it a day, and I could seriously use a beer."

We end up at a cozy restaurant called Coppi's on U Street that has great wood-fired pizza and a couple decent beers on tap. We nibble on pizza and talk a little about our families. Alex tells me that she grew up in Denver, has three younger sisters and everyone in her family is an avid skier. She reluctantly admits that her real name is Alaska.

"Apparently, that's where I was conceived and my parents thought the name was cute," she says with a laugh. "But growing up, most kids thought it was weird, and I've gone by Alex for as long as I can remember."

"Well, at least your parents didn't give you an old lady name like Matilda," I reply.

"Is that your real name?" Alex tries to suppress a giggle.

"Unfortunately! But don't even think about calling me that. I may never speak to you again," I say kiddingly.

"Ditto with Alaska!"

"Is most of your family still in the Denver area?" I ask as I grab the last piece of pizza.

"Yeah, everyone is still there, except me, of course. But I see them all as much as I can. My sister Walker is the youngest, but even though we're the furthest apart in age, she and I are especially close. I talk to her a few times a week. She's a nurse in Denver, and she spends every free moment skiing and hiking with her boyfriend and their three dogs." She pauses and looks up at me. "So what is your story? Where did you grow up?"

I pause before answering. I want to tell her as much of the truth as I can. "I grew up in Vermont, but I don't have any immediate family there anymore, both my parents are dead. They were a lot older when I was born. Anyway, my dad had his own accounting business, which—not surprisingly—is how I got interested in the profession, but he was practically retired by the time I got to high school. My mom was an artist. She dabbled in sculpture and painting, but her true passion was pottery. She made some really beautiful things."

"Do you have any siblings?"

"Ah, yes…" I let out a big sigh and tell her about my not-so-beloved sister Abby while I play with the leftover pizza crusts on my plate.

"That's really a shame," Alex says when I tell her that Abby has basically cut off all ties with me. "Some people can be so small-minded, it just kills me. In my opinion, life is just too short to simply cut people out of your life without truly trying to understand them."

I nod. "Yeah, I agree. It makes me really sad sometimes. I guess maybe I should try harder to reach out to her, and who knows? Maybe she'll come around someday. I'm jealous that you have such a close relationship with your sisters."

After dinner, we walk down Sixteenth Street, a beautiful, tree-lined thoroughfare that runs straight from the White House to the Maryland border, until we reach Q Street. Given the location of our respective homes, it makes sense for us to part ways at Sixteenth and Q.

Alex stops walking and turns to me. "Well, I guess this is where we go our separate ways. Goodnight, Mattie, I had a really nice evening." She reaches over to give me a friendly hug good-bye.

My body trembles slightly at being in such close proximity to her. "Goodnight, Alex. Yeah, me too, I really enjoyed hearing about your family."

As I walk home, I smile as I think back to our evening together. Alex's so easy to be with, and she's incredibly beautiful. I readily acknowledge that I am most definitely developing a serious crush on her. God, I just feel so drawn to Alex whenever I'm near her. But I know there are countless reasons why a relationship with Alex is so not happening. I need to accept that. The sooner I do, the better. Under no circumstances can I let her know how I feel. Easier said than done, I think to myself.

* * *

By the end of the week, I'm ready to walk Alex through all the Hemlock finances. Everything is updated, and I developed some good spreadsheets to make it easier to track accounts, invoices, and expenses. Alex and I set up a block of time to meet on Friday afternoon. We sit down in her office, and I start to show her what I've done so far. She seems impressed and can't believe what I have accomplished in such a short time.

"You are a complete and utter Excel wizard!" she declares.

"Well, thanks. The spreadsheets should make things easier, but honestly, I think Hemlock needs to invest in some sort of accounting software. It would make it much easier to really dig into the numbers and identify areas of opportunity and strength, and also to pinpoint areas of weakness. I know you do what you do because you love it, but I can help you maximize your profit."

"When you talk like that, I am inclined to listen to you!" She chuckles and then thanks me profusely.

We agree to discuss the financials further the following week, and I start to gather up my stuff and head out of her office when she places a soft hand on my shoulder.

"Can I make you dinner to thank you for all your awesome work?" she asks.

I remind her that she's paying me to work at Hemlock and that she's already had me to dinner once, but she won't take no for an answer. So I suggest a compromise, "I will let you make me dinner if you let me buy the groceries *and* the wine."

"Okay, I suppose that's reasonable." She pouts. "What do you say we blow this popsicle stand?"

We lock up at Hemlock and walk toward Alex's loft, making a quick pit stop at Whole Foods on the way to pick up some wine and food for dinner. We decide to keep the menu simple: steak and salad. Once we get back to her place, I chop up vegetables for the salad while Alex fires up the grill and sets the table.

It's a chilly night, but I join Alex outside to keep her company while she grills the steaks. The sun is setting over the city, and I can see the last of the light bouncing off the Washington Monument in the distance.

When dinner's ready, I open the nice bottle of cabernet sauvignon we picked up at Whole Foods and pour us each a glass. Alex digs some candles out of a drawer, lights them and dims the kitchen lights before we finally sit down to eat.

"Mmmmm…this steak is perfectly cooked, Alex," I say after I swallow my first bite.

"Thanks. It's funny, in most couples the man is usually the grill master, but when Robert was alive, I always grilled while he made the side dishes. My dad is like Mr. Grill. I think he and my mom grill out at least five nights a week. Anyway, when I was growing up, he taught me the art!" she says with a laugh.

"Well, lucky me. I wouldn't even know how to turn a grill on. I don't think my parents even owned one."

After dinner, we both do the dishes. I pour us each a little more wine before following Alex into the living room. She starts a fire in the fireplace and joins me on the sofa. As we chat, I do my best to stay focused on the conversation as I fight the urge to reach out and touch her. I can't help it. Being around her feels incredible, and I desperately want something more. My vow to keep my feelings to myself is proving extremely difficult. I need to get the hell out of there before I do something that I regret.

"It's getting late. I should probably head home. Thank you for a wonderful evening," I say reluctantly as I set my half-empty wineglass on the coffee table and stand up.

"Are you sure you don't want to stay and finish your wine?"

"I'd love to, but I think I had a little too much of that delicious steak and my stomach is protesting."

"Yeah, I hear you. Between the two of us, I think we ate enough steak to feed a family of six." She laughs.

I carry my wineglass into the kitchen and set it in the sink while Alex pulls my coat out of the front hall closet. "What are you doing Sunday?" she asks as she hands me my coat.

"Um, nothing much. Why, what do you have in mind?"

"Well, I know it's freezing outside right now, but there's a warm front headed toward DC and it's supposed to be unseasonably warm and sunny on Sunday. And, well, I was thinking about going for a mountain bike ride. Any interest in joining me?"

"Yeah, definitely. I love mountain biking. Oh, but my mountain bike is in Vermont."

"I've got two—you can use one of mine. Robert bought me a sweet new bike the Christmas before he died, but I still have my old bike and it's pretty good too. There's a trail that I love in Virginia if you don't mind a little bit of a drive?"

"No, that sounds awesome. Count me in!"

"Okay, cool. How about I swing by and pick you up around eight o'clock Sunday morning?"

"Sounds good, but only if you let me pack lunch."

CHAPTER TWENTY-TWO

Alex pulls up in front of my apartment at promptly eight o'clock Sunday morning, and I can see that she's got two bikes loaded in the back of her pickup truck.

"Good morning! Gosh, you were right, it is a beautiful day. I can't believe how warm it is," I say as I climb up into the passenger seat.

"Good morning to you too. Yeah, I'm pretty pumped to get out for a ride."

"So, where exactly are we headed?"

"Well, the trail I mentioned on Friday night is located about halfway between DC and Charlottesville. The ride is really pretty, but it is a bit of a climb. Are up for that?"

"Yeah, I think so. God knows running with you has whipped my sorry ass into shape."

"Good!" She laughs. "We haven't gotten much snow so far this winter so I'm hoping that the trail will be pretty dry."

The drive to the trail takes about an hour and a half, but I don't really mind. We drive through beautiful countryside, and it feels good to be out of the city for a change. It's nearly sixty degrees by the time we park the truck near the trail. We jump out of the truck and start to organize our gear. Alex tinkers with her old bike to make sure that it's adjusted properly for me. Eventually, we set off down a bumpy dirt road toward the bike trail.

The trail itself is a single track that winds and climbs through a heavily forested area. I do the best I can to keep up with Alex while admiring her cute ass. Damn, she looks good in bike clothes, I think to myself on multiple occasions.

After riding for nearly two hours, we stop at a small clearing near the top of a rolling hill so we can sit and have lunch in the sun. It's an absolutely incredible day for February—the sky is clear and we can see for miles across the valley.

I unpack a container of chicken salad I made along with some cheese and crackers plus two bottles of Gatorade and set everything out on the ground in front of us. We quickly devour the food, and I finish off my bottle of Gatorade before lying back on the grass and closing my eyes to enjoy the warmth of the sun.

Alex lies down next to me and plants a quick kiss on my cheek. I look up at her in surprise, and she's staring down at me with those beautiful green eyes. I smile up at her with a questioning look, and she leans down and kisses me softly on the lips. I put my hand behind her head, and she needs no further encouragement to deepen the kiss. My head is swimming as I feel her tongue tentatively seek out mine. When she finally pulls back, all I can do is stare up at her in disbelief.

"Where did that come from? Not that I'm complaining," I manage.

She stares back at me for a moment before responding. "Oh, Mattie…I've got a serious thing for you."

"A thing?" I ask and swallow hard. My heart feels like it might jump out of my chest.

"A crush. I have a major crush on you."

"You do? But I don't understand. You're…"

"I dated a few women before I met Robert…" She trails off.

"Oh," is all I can manage. I feel like I need to pinch myself to make sure I'm not dreaming.

Alex leans down and gives me another quick kiss on the lips. "And to think that I have been fighting the urge to kiss you for weeks now." I laugh after she pulls away.

"You have?"

"Yeah," I admit with a smile. "I think I've had a thing for you since we bumped into each other at Kramer's. I've been doing my best to try to contain my feelings, and it wasn't easy, let me tell you," I say with a laugh. "But I thought you were straight and I love spending time with you and I didn't want to jeopardize our friendship…"

"Well, it just so happens that I started having feelings for you that day at Kramer's too. I just wanted to take some time to get to know you better before I…um…pursued anything. I mean, of course I didn't know for sure that the feelings were mutual but I, um, did detect a few signs…"

I laugh at her nervous ramble. "And all this time I thought I was doing such a good job hiding the fact that I was crazy attracted to you," I say with a sly smile.

She lets out a hearty laugh, gives me one last quick kiss and then stands up and reaches down to pull me to my feet. "We better head back to the truck. After all, it's only February and it'll get chilly once the sun starts to set."

The bike ride back to the parking lot is mostly either downhill or flat, and we get back to the truck in less than an hour. We load the bikes into the back of the truck and hit the road back to DC. It doesn't take long before I doze off, and when I finally wake up, the sun has nearly set.

I rub my eyes and look over at Alex. She smiles back at me, causing my breath to catch. How did I get so damn lucky? After all that happened in the last few months, it doesn't seem possible that I found someone like Alex. I actually feel a little guilty for feeling so happy.

It's well after dark by the time we get back to DC. We discuss going out to grab a beer, but we're both beat from the long ride and Alex has a meeting with a potential new client early the next morning up near Baltimore. She parks her truck outside my apartment and reaches up to cup my cheek and places a soft kiss on my lips.

"See you at the office tomorrow afternoon?" she says when she pulls back.

I'm still relishing the feel of her lips on mine as I nod and reluctantly climb out of her warm truck. She waves as she pulls away from the curb, and I practically skip up the walkway to my apartment.

CHAPTER TWENTY-THREE

Alex doesn't get back to the office until late Monday morning after her meeting in Baltimore. I'm downright giddy when I run into her in the break room, and I give her a goofy grin.

"Hey," she says and treats me to a broad smile. Her green eyes twinkle.

"Hey, how'd the meeting in Baltimore go?" I ask.

"Fine. Actually, more than fine. I think we landed a big new client."

"Awesome."

"I had a really good time yesterday," Alex says shyly.

A big smile crosses my face. "Yeah, me too."

Just then Renee, the receptionist walks into the break room to fill her coffee mug. Alex gives her a quick hello and excuses herself to run to another client meeting.

The rest of the day is crazy busy in the office, and I don't see her again before I have to leave for the day. I have to skip out early because my neighbor Stella has invited me to a concert at the Kennedy Center and I need to change into something more respectable before I meet her. Last week I took Stella to a doctor's appointment and changed some light bulbs in her apartment and she's taking me to the concert to thank me.

Stella has season tickets for the National Symphony Orchestra, and the ushers at the Kennedy Center all seem to know her by name. I note that the program for the evening includes Beethoven's *Eighth Symphony* and Tchaikovsky's *Serenade for Strings*.

"It's one of my favorites," Stella whispers in my ear as we take our seats.

I look over at Stella just as the music begins, and she has the biggest grin on her face. I'm not a classical music aficionado by any stretch of the imagination, but it's nice to see Stella so happy. Both of her daughters live in California and don't visit very often. I know she gets lonely.

It's still fairly early when I get home from the concert so I change into jeans and a T-shirt, pour myself a glass of wine and flip on the news. I plop down on the couch just as my phone vibrates to indicate that I have an incoming text. I reach for my phone and have a big grin on my face when I see that it's from Alex.

Sorry I barely got to see you today. How was the concert?

Great, we had a really nice time, I respond before quickly typing another message. *Will you have dinner with me tomorrow night?*

Are you asking me out on a date?

Yes, I am.

She sends back a smiley face, and I take that as a yes.

* * *

The next night, I take Alex out to dinner at a small French place in Woodley Park. It's a neighborhood place that's been around forever. I'm pleased when the hostess leads us to a nice, cozy candlelit table in the front corner of the restaurant. We look over the menu and decide to be brave and order escargot to share for an appetizer. I order steak frites for my main dish, and Alex chooses the Scottish salmon. The waiter suggests a bottle of wine for us to split.

Alex reaches across the table and curls our fingers together. "It's nice to be on a real live date with you. I'm glad I finally came to my senses and kissed you," Alex says softly.

"Me too."

"This place is amazing. You sure know how to order up the romance," she says teasingly.

"I wanted our first official date to be special," I say seriously.

"Whenever I'm with you, it feels special." She looks into my eyes.

I feel like I might pass out. "Me too," I say shakily.

We continue to smile dumbly at each other until the waiter reappears with the bottle of wine we ordered. I let Alex taste the wine, and once she gives her approval, the waiter pours us each a glass before walking off to the next table. We linger over our entrees and order a cheese plate to share for desert.

Alex offers to pay half the bill, but I insist on paying for dinner. "I asked you out, remember?" I say.

We stop by the coat check on our way out, and the valet offers to hail us a taxi. Normally, I would prefer to walk, but it's cold and windy outside so I reply, "Yes, please," as we follow him out to the street. The valet blows his whistle and a taxi appears out of nowhere.

"Where to?" the driver asks when we climb in the taxi.

Alex and I look at each other. "1445 Church Street in Logan Circle," she says quickly before turning back to me. "Would you like to come to my place for a nightcap?" she asks.

"Twist my arm!" I say with a smile.

She looks up at me and starts to say something, but before she gets the chance, her cell phone rings. She pulls her phone from her purse and glances at the caller ID and looks up at me apologetically. "It's Karen. I've got to pick up. She and Doug have been having issues, and it's unlike her to call this late." Karen is Alex's best friend. I met her and her boyfriend Doug at Alex's dinner party back in January.

I nod that I understand, and she answers the call. "Hey, Kar. Is everything all right? We're just getting back from din... Oh, sweetie, I'm sorry." She puts her hand over the phone and whispers to me. "She's sobbing. She and Doug broke up. I'm afraid that nightcap is going to have to wait."

"Oh, poor thing!"

She mouths "Sorry" before giving me a quick peck on the cheek and climbing out of the taxi. I give her hand a squeeze and mouth back "It's okay" before directing the taxi driver to my apartment.

My phone vibrates the second I walk in the door of my apartment. I dig my phone out of my pocket and see that it's a text from Todd. *Hey Mattie. I am headed down to NYC on Friday for a business meeting. Any chance you and Ellen can get together Saturday? Would love to see you both.*

I text him back right away. *Works for me! Let me call Ellen and get back to you. Would love to see you too!*

I take off my coat and give Ellen a quick call to see if she's free for dinner on Saturday. She is, so I text Todd back to confirm that the three of us are on for dinner on Saturday in New York.

I brush my teeth, change into my pajamas and climb into bed with a book. Before I manage to read three sentences, my phone rings. It's Alex, so I pick up. "Hey, you. How's Karen?"

"Oh God, she's a total mess. She was so sure that Doug was *the one*. I don't know though, they've only been together for a few months and I never felt the "vibe" between them, if you know what I mean? Anyway, I guess he accepted a job in Dallas without even consulting her, and, well…you can imagine that didn't go over very well. I think she'll be okay though, she's a really tough cookie. I, on the other hand, am very sorry that our exceptionally wonderful date had to come to such an abrupt end."

"Me too," I whisper, smiling into the phone.

"Can I make it up to you by cooking dinner for you on Friday night?" she asks hopefully.

"Yeah, that would be wonderful."

"Okay, great. Night, Mattie."

"Night, Alex."

CHAPTER TWENTY-FOUR

Alex swings by my desk on Friday afternoon and explains she has to run out to a jobsite and probably won't make it back to the office before the end of the day. "We're still on for dinner tonight, right?" she asks as she casually rests her hand on my shoulder.

"I wouldn't miss it for the world."

"Cool, why don't you come by my place around seven o'clock? Does that work?" she asks.

I nod, and she turns to run off to her appointment.

I arrive at Alex's apartment a little after seven that evening, and she buzzes me up. Amazing aromas greet me as I step off the elevator on her floor. I knock softly on her door, and she answers wearing an apron and one oven mitt. I chuckle when I see that she has some sort of black liquid smeared on her cheek. She looks adorable.

"Hi, sweetie," she says and gives me a quick peck on the lips before closing the door behind me. "I am trying a new recipe, and I think it may be a little out of my league!"

I laugh. "Trying to impress me, huh?" I reach over and wipe the black substance off her cheek with one of my fingers. "I guess that explains why part of dinner is stuck to your face," I say with a smirk.

"Oh, God. How embarrassing!" She laughs. "Come on in and pour yourself some wine. I've got to stir the concoction on the stove before it burns."

I do as directed and then join her next to the stove. "Anything I can do to help?"

"Nah, I think I have it under control," she says while she pours the black concoction over what looks like pasta and vegetables in a baking dish and then slides the whole thing into the oven. She sets the timer and then unties her apron and tosses it on the counter. "Dinner should be ready in about thirty minutes. Whether it's edible remains to be seen!"

I take a seat on the couch in the living room while Alex expertly starts a fire in the fireplace. Once the fire is roaring, she joins me on the couch we chat about DC politics, the weather and a new exhibit at the Phillips Collection that we both want to see. The oven timer interrupts us thirty minutes later, and we head back into the kitchen. Alex pulls the casserole from the oven and puts the final touches on dinner while I set the table and light some candles.

She carries the baking dish over to the table andscoops a big heap of the black casserole onto each of our plates before setting the baking dish on the counter and joining me at the table. We both stare at our plates hesitantly.

"All right, I'm going in!" I pick up my fork and shovel some of the black mixture into my mouth. Alex looks at me expectantly as I finish chewing. I laugh because she looks so damn earnest. "It's really, *really* good," I finally assure her.

She gives me a skeptical look and cautiously picks up her fork to taste the meal she's created. "Wow, you're right, that is pretty damn good!" she says proudly after she's swallowed her first bite.

After dinner, I help Alex with the dishes. When we're done, she wanders into the living room to add a log to the waning fire and then gestures me toward the couch. She sits down close to me and pulls a wool blanket up over us. We curl up together and watch the flames of the fire in silence.

Eventually, Alex slips her arm around my shoulder and pulls me even closer. She leans in and starts placing soft kisses on my lips. I greet them eagerly, and it doesn't take long for the heat to build between us. Alex slips her tongue into my mouth, and I groan with pleasure. We kiss slowly but passionately, and when Alex pulls back, her gaze is full of desire. She reaches down and pulls my sweater up over my head before attacking my mouth with renewed hunger. As we kiss, she runs her fingers over the silk of my bra. My nipples come to immediate attention, and I feel a strong pull in my groin.

Alex pauses to reach back and unhook my bra. I take this opportunity to push her down gently on the couch and shift my position so that I'm straddling her waist. I look down into her eyes and slowly start to unbutton her blouse. While I work on her buttons, she reaches up to tease my nipples with her fingers. I am humming, and I feel like my body might explode.

I finally get her blouse undone and push it back so that I can smooth my hands over her toned stomach and up over the black lace bra that barely covers her ample breasts. Her nipples harden under my touch, and she moans contentedly before pulling me down into yet another mind-blowing kiss. Our tongues lash together, and I reach back to release her bra. Her breasts spill out, and I bring my mouth down to taste them…but then reality sets in. I release her nipple from my mouth and sit up abruptly.

"Don't stop," Alex moans.

"I can't do this, Alex."

Her mouth opens, but nothing comes out.

"I haven't been honest with you," I say as I blow out a deep breath.

Alex shifts beneath me and stares up at me with those amazing green eyes, but she remains silent, waiting to hear what I have to say.

"I'm in DC because I am on the run. I mean, I'm not a full-fledged outlaw or anything," I say quickly.

"I don't understand." She reaches for the wool blanket on the back of the couch and tugs it around her exposed torso.

I pick my sweater up off the floor and pull it back over my head before sitting back down to tell Alex about my past. I take a deep breath before I begin. I've never told anyone about what I did. I've never cared enough about someone to risk telling them the truth. With Alex, it's different. It's worth the risk.

I give her all the highlights. I tell her I used to be an art thief and I tell her that I've been on the run since December when a burglary went particularly bad. "I lost two of my best friends," I explain. "They died during the course of the burglary."

She seems taken aback when I tell her about Kat and Sarah, but for the most part, she just stares at me with utter disbelief as I explain how I came to be in DC.

"Wow," is all she says when I'm done.

I try to explain that I've hung up my thief hat for good, but it seems to fall on deaf ears. I'm completely crestfallen and instinctively wrap my arms around myself.

Alex stands and walks toward the windows. "I'm not sure what to say."

"You don't need to say anything. I am so sorry, I should have told you sooner," I say as I stand and walk toward her front door. "I should go."

Alex walks over toward the front door as I'm grabbing my coat out of the closet. I slip on my coat and turn to face her. "I'm sorry," I say again in a whisper as I fight back tears.

"I need some time to absorb all this," she says finally.

"I understand. It's a lot to absorb."

I head out the door, and tears well up in my eyes.

CHAPTER TWENTY-FIVE

The next morning, I take the Acela train back up to New York to have dinner with Todd and Ellen. I've talked to Todd on the phone once or twice over the last few months, but this is the first time Ellen and I have seen him since the Schuyler House.

Todd is already at Ellen's when I arrive and I break down the second I see him. He pulls me into a hug and starts crying too. Eventually, I step back. "I'm the one that should be hugging you, you big dummy. How are you holding up?"

"Ah, okay. It sucks though. I miss her so damn much."

This time, I pull him into my arms and Ellen comes over and wraps her arms around both of us. "Group hug," she says.

"I miss her too," I say when we pull apart.

The three of us sit around Ellen's apartment for the next hour and talk about the "good ole days." I've spent so much time being angry and sad about what happened. So much time missing Sarah and Kat and feeling guilty that they died. It feels good to talk and laugh about them, to remember some of the good times we had.

"Well, we should probably head to dinner. Our reservation is in fifteen minutes and it will take us about ten minutes to walk there," Ellen says eventually.

Once we place our order, we get down to business. We begin to discuss what to do with the cash that remains in the safe deposit box and with the money still in the Hatshepsut Consulting checking account.

"I checked the balance of the Hatshepsut checking account online a few days ago and it still has something like $450,000 in it," Ellen says. "And even after Mattie and I raided the safe deposit box, I think there is still at least $250,000 left in that," she adds.

"Shit, that is a lot of money," Todd remarks.

We talk over a bunch of options but eventually agree to split the remaining money into three piles. First, we will set aside $250,000 as a college fund for Sarah's kids. Second, we will donate $250,000 to an environmental conservation fund in Vermont about which Kat was extremely passionate. Lastly, we decide to leave the last $200,000 in the Hatshepsut account for future emergencies. None of us says it, but we all know that "future emergencies" is code for "if we get caught and need to hire a lawyer."

After dinner, we make plans to meet up the next morning for a run. Todd heads back to his hotel, and Ellen and I walk back to her apartment.

"Up for a little after dinner drink?" Ellen asks once we get back to her place.

"Sure, why not?"

"I've got some whiskey that will put some serious hair on your chest," she says with a laugh as she pulls two glasses out from a cabinet in the kitchen. She pours a little bit of brown liquid in each glass and hands me one.

I sit down on one of the stools at her kitchen island and take a tentative sip of the whiskey. "Wow, shit, you weren't kidding about the hair on the chest stuff!"

She laughs and then gets a serious look on her face. "How do you feel about the way we decided to split up the money?"

"I think I feel pretty good about it, all things considered. What about you?"

"I feel pretty good about it too. I know Jake doesn't make much money, and I want to make sure Sarah's kids can go to college without having to rack up mounds of debt since I know that was something Sarah was always concerned about…and I think, if she were alive, Kat would approve of the donation to the conservation fund."

I nod, and we sit quietly for a while and sip our whiskey. I let out a big yawn, and Ellen looks at me understandingly. "Yeah, I'm beat too. What do you say we hit the hay?"

Ellen helps me make up the pull-out couch in her living room and wishes me goodnight before disappearing into her room. I get ready for bed, turn out the lights and climb into bed. I am exhausted but can't seem to fall asleep. All I can do is think about Alex. I know I'm falling in love with her and I'm petrified she will decide she never wants to see me again. I flip about under the covers and try to resist the urge to call her, finally succumbing to sleep.

Ellen and I both sleep in the next morning. We finally make our way over to Central Park around ten o'clock to meet Todd for a run. There is something special about running in Central Park. The city closes off all the roads inside the park to cars on the weekends, and they fill with runners, bikers, Rollerbladers, and people just out for a stroll. The people watching is amazing, and it's wonderful to be in such a lush, green space in the middle of one of the biggest cities in the world. After we run, Ellen and I bid Todd farewell. He's taking the train back to Vermont that afternoon. Ellen and I grab a late breakfast before heading back to her apartment to shower.

Ellen jumps in the shower first, and I pick up my phone while I wait my turn. My heart skips a beat when I see that I have a missed call and a voice mail from Alex. Her message doesn't say much except that she will try and call again later. I call her back right away, but it goes straight to voice mail so I leave a message, "Hey, it's Mattie. I got your message. Sorry I missed you. I was out running. I'm in New York visiting friends, but I will be back in DC soon…I can't stop thinking about you, Alex."

Ellen and I are supposed to meet Andy and Sandy at six o'clock for dinner and drinks, and we decide to just lounge around her apartment and read the Sunday *New York Times* until we have to get ready. Not long after we've settled into the couch with the paper, my phone chirps. I grab it right away and look at the caller ID. It's Alex. I turn to Ellen. "I need to take this. I'm going to step out on the balcony."

Once I'm outside, I accept the call and say "Hi" softly.

"Hi. I've been trying to reach you…to tell you…that I can't see you anymore, Mattie," Alex says. "I'm sorry."

"But…I…" I stutter.

"I'm sorry," Alex says again. "I've given it a lot of thought, and I keep coming up with the same answer. I've been through so much the last couple of years, and this is just more than I can swallow right now. And I think it's best that you stop working at Hemlock…I hope you understand."

I try to speak, but nothing comes out.

"Good-bye, Mattie," Alex says quietly.

"Alex, please…" But it's too late. She's ended the call.

I stuff the phone in my pocket and just stare at the street below. A tear trickles down my cheek. I'm cold, but I don't care. After a few minutes, I pull my phone back out and tap Alex's number. It rings once, but I quickly end the call before she picks up. I tell myself I've got to respect her decision. I knew that there were consequences to being a thief, and this is certainly one of them. I jam the phone back in my pocket and turn to open the balcony door.

Ellen looks up from her paper when I step back inside. A look of concern crosses her face. "What's wrong Mattie?" she asks.

"Nothing," I say.

Ellen just looks at me. She knows something's up, and she's not going to let me off that easy.

"All right. Well, there's this…um, woman in DC. Her name is Alex and she…" I only get that far before I begin sobbing.

Ellen gets up off the couch. She wraps her arms around me, and I sob into her shoulder. Eventually, Ellen leads me to the couch. I slump into it while she runs to grab a box of tissue from the bathroom. "Tell me what happened," Ellen says when she returns and joins me on the couch.

I tell her the whole story about Alex and the accounting work I've been doing for Hemlock. Then I tell her what happened the night before I left for New York. "I knew it was a risk to tell her the truth, but I didn't feel like I had a choice," I say before pausing to catch my breath. "Anyway, that was her on the phone. She called to tell me that she doesn't want to see me anymore. Can't say I blame her."

"Oh, sweetie. I'm sorry," Ellen says. She's silent for a minute before adding, "Do you trust her?"

It takes me a minute to digest her question. "Yeah, I do," I say finally, and I mean it. I haven't known Alex all that long, but somehow, I just don't see her running to the police. "And don't worry, I didn't give her any names or anything," I add.

Ellen pats my leg. "How about a little ice cream to cheer you up?"

I saddle up to her kitchen island and Ellen pulls a container of ice cream out of the freezer and hands a spoon. "No bowls?" I ask.

"I hate doing dishes," she says with a laugh as she jabs her spoon into the container of mint chip. We polish off about half the container in no time. "Feel any better?" Ellen asks as she puts what's left of the ice cream back in the freezer.

"No, not really," I confess. "God, El, I really like her. It just sucks."

"You're welcome to stay here as long as you want," Ellen offers.

"Thanks."

CHAPTER TWENTY-SIX

I spend nearly a week moping around Ellen's apartment. She's gone most of the day, and I mostly just sit around and channel surf. I try to drag myself out for a walk around the neighborhood every day, but my energy level is so low that I find the walks almost painful, which is so incredibly strange for me. I've always been Ms. High Energy. Normally, I'm bouncing off the walls if I go even one day without exercise.

Finally, I decide it's time to head back to DC. I've probably already overstayed my welcome at Ellen's, and I know I need to stop hiding out in her apartment and figure out what's next for me.

Ellen takes me out to a wine bar in her neighborhood my last night in New York, and I have about three too many glasses of sauvignon blanc. I'm totally hung over the next morning and have to drag myself out of bed to catch my train. The noise and whirlwind of activity in Penn Station causes my head to throb. I make a beeline for the "quiet car" when it's time to board the train and sleep almost the entire three-hour ride back to DC.

I climb the stairs up to my apartment and set my bag down outside my door while I fish for my keys. Just then, Stella's door opens and she pops her head out into the hallway. It's like she was sitting by the door listening for me. She probably was.

"Hi Mattie," she says cheerfully. "You've been away for an awfully long time."

"Hi Stella," I say somewhat wearily, although the nap on the train did wonders for my hangover. "Yeah, I was away a lot longer than I expected."

"Well, it's nice to have you back home," she says with a sweet smile.

"Thanks," I say as I finally locate my keys and stand to put them in the door. I turn back to Stella before opening my door. "I've got to run to the grocery store this afternoon. Can I get you anything?"

"No, dear, but thank you."

"Okay, well, let me know if you need anything."

"Well, now that you mention it, I am having a bit of an issue with my computer. Would you mind stopping by tomorrow to take a look at it?"

"Not at all. I'll stop by in the morning," I say.

"Oh, Mattie, you're such a dear."

"My pleasure. See you tomorrow Stella," I say as I step inside my apartment and close the door.

Suddenly, I feel extremely lonely. I've always liked my apartment but now it just feels claustrophobic and depressing. I plop on the sofa and look around the space. It is totally devoid of anything personal. Even the refrigerator magnets look lonely because they've nothing to hold. I put my hands over my face and start to cry.

* * *

I spend much of the next few days helping Stella with her computer and a few light handyman projects around her house. It's funny. I know she's lonely, and I think she sometimes makes up things for me to do just so she'll have my company. But, right now, I think I need her company even more than she needs mine. She invites me to another concert at the Kennedy Center. The concert is not until the following week, but I still practically jump at the chance to join her.

Although I'm managing to keep myself fairly busy during the day, my evenings are quiet and feel painfully long. I kill time watching TV and surfing the Internet. Anything to avoid thinking about Alex and about my future. Finally, one night I crack. I can't take it anymore. I've got to get out of the house. I take a quick shower and head to Tina's, the most popular lesbian bar in DC.

The bar is totally packed when I arrive. I order a beer at the bar and take a few healthy swigs of it while I scan the crowd. Most of the patrons are younger than me, and it seems like everyone is coupled up. I polish off the rest of my beer, order a second one and wander over toward a group of women playing pool.

"Up for a game?" a woman asks. She's fairly attractive and nearly my age.

"Sure, why not? But I have to warn you, I pretty much suck at pool," I reply.

"Don't worry. None of us are very good." She hands me a cue stick. "By the way, my name's Chloe," she says, and extends a hand.

"Mattie," I reply. "Nice to meet you."

One game turns into four or five games with a few trips to the bar in between. I've got a serious buzz by the time Chloe and I set down our pool sticks and head for the dance floor. The music is thumping. At first, Chloe and I dance loosely with a group of women, but by the second or third song, Chloe's got her arms around me and we're bumping and grinding.

"Wanna get out of here?" she asks finally.

I nod, and she takes my hand and leads me out of the bar. We walk a few blocks to her apartment and practically rip each other's clothes off the second we're inside. We end up having sex right on her living room couch.

Afterward, Chloe pads into the kitchen and gets us both a beer.

"Thanks, I say when she hands me one although I don't really want it. I suddenly feel hollow and I know I've already had too much to drink. I pull a blanket off the back of the couch and drape it over my naked body.

"So, do you go to Tina's a lot?" Chloe asks.

"No," I reply a little more curtly than I intend. I feel badly. It's not Chloe's fault. She seems like a nice person. I'm just not really up for small talk.

Chloe flips on the TV. I stare at it for a while, not really seeing what's on the screen. "I should go," I blurt out eventually.

"But the night is young," Chloe protests.

"I know, I'm sorry, but I need to leave."

I stand and begin to gather my clothes that were tossed hastily onto the floor.

Chloe pulls on a shirt and walks me to the door. "I had a nice time. Hope I see you around Tina's again soon."

"Um, yeah, me too." I give her a weak smile before I open the door and step outside. "Bye, Chloe."

* * *

I walk home slowly and chastise myself for going home with Chloe. If anything, I now feel even more depressed. I've had maybe two one-night stands in my whole life. I'm not really even sure why I went to Tina's.

I round the corner onto Q Street and see flashing red lights down the block. As I get closer to my apartment, I realize an ambulance is parked outside my building. I pick up my pace and step into the lobby of my building just as the paramedics are getting off the elevator with Stella.

"Oh my gosh. What happened?" I ask no one in particular.

"She had a fall. Could be a broken hip," one of the paramedics replies as they maneuver Stella through the front door.

I watch as they wheel her down the walk to the waiting ambulance, and I feel utterly alone. I bow my head and begin to trudge up the stairs to my apartment. My legs feel like bricks, and I'm winded when I reach my landing.

CHAPTER TWENTY-SEVEN

I go to visit Stella a few times while she's in the hospital. The first time I visit she is pretty drugged up, but when I go back a few days later, she's much more alert and back to her chatty self. It sounds like she'll be transferred to an assisted-living facility soon.

"I'm not staying there long!" she assures me. "I'm going home as soon as I can."

"I like your attitude," I reply.

She goes on to tell me that her older daughter is on her way in from LA and she seems very excited to see her. Stella and I are supposed to go to the Kennedy Center together the following evening, and she insists I take her tickets and go on my own.

"I'd hate for them to go to waste," she says. "I pay good money for them. Take a friend if you like."

"Thanks, Stella," I reply. "I'm just sorry you can't join me."

She gives me a smile, and I can tell she's tired. I excuse myself and promise to visit her again soon.

* * *

The next evening, I attend the concert solo. I find the music incredibly calming, and when the concert lets out, I feel more myself than I have in weeks. It's a nice evening, so I decide to walk the mile or so back to my apartment.

I turn up the front walk of my apartment building and immediately notice the silhouette of a person sitting on the front stoop. I'm a bit startled and stop walking.

"Mattie?" a familiar voice asks.

"Alex, is that you?" I say softly.

The silhouette stands and starts to walk toward me. As it gets closer, I'm able to make out Alex's face in the faint light.

"What are you doing here?" I ask.

Alex doesn't say anything. She just wraps her arms around me and rests her head on my shoulder. Tentatively, I place my arms around her waist. Her body feels so good against mine.

After a few moments, Alex lifts her head and looks at me. "I was so worried that you were gone. I tried to call you and it went straight to voice mail, so I decided to walk over here and see if you were home. I rang your bell a few times, and when I got no response, I started to wonder if maybe you'd decided to stay in New York for good."

"I was at the Kennedy Center and I had my phone turned off. I forgot to turn it back on after the concert…"

"Do you mind if we go inside and talk?" Alex interrupts me.

"Um, sure."

I feel both anxious and cautiously optimistic as we make our way up to my apartment.

Alex sits down on the couch in my living room, and I perch myself on a nearby chair. My brain is prepared for the worst while my heart is full of hope.

"I've missed you so much," Alex starts. "I know I said that coming to grips with your past was more than I could handle right now, but…I've come to realize that being without you is much worse. I want you in my life but first, I need to know if you, um, plan to keep at it?"

"Keep at what?"

"Stealing art."

Oddly, my first reaction is to laugh. I think my emotions at this point are completely out of whack. Thankfully, I manage to suppress that urge and instead take a deep breath before answering her. "Not in a million years."

"Are you sure?" Alex asks.

I nod and try to explain to her what it was like to lose two of my closest friends and how I now realize how stupid we were. "Sadly, it took the catastrophe at Schuyler House to bring me to my senses," I say finally.

"Well, I'm certainly relieved that you don't intend to continue that way of life. I needed to hear you say that. I'm just sorry that it took something so horrible to finally make you stop," Alex responds.

I stand up from my chair and join her on the couch. We hold each other for a long time. Finally, I pull back and look up at her. "I can't tell you how miserable I've been the last few weeks. I was a complete mess when you told me that you couldn't see me anymore. I wanted to call you like a million times, but I knew I had to respect your decision."

Alex gives me a soft kiss on the lips. I take it as a confirmation of what's been said. A confirmation that we're going to try and move beyond my past together.

"It's late. I should go," she says.

"Okay," I say as we both stand.

"Up for a run tomorrow?" she asks as I walk her to the door.

"Definitely!"

"Usual spot, seven a.m.?"

"I'll be there!"

That night I go to bed and feel happier than I have in my whole life.

CHAPTER TWENTY-EIGHT

The next morning is beautiful, and Alex and I run our first mile mostly in silence. I feel like I am on cloud nine. Our pace is fast, and I have no problem keeping it up.

"How are things at Hemlock?" I ask finally.

"Good, but crazy busy," Alex replies. "I'm loath to say we've almost got too much work."

"I'm glad to hear things are going well."

"Any chance you'd consider coming back to work?" she asks.

"Are you kidding? I'd love to! I love working at Hemlock. There is so much good energy in the office, and it makes me feel useful."

"It would be really good to have you back," Alex says. "You've been a godsend with the books and I miss having you around the office."

"Would today be too soon to restart?" I ask.

Alex lets out a laugh. "No!"

"Great, I look forward to it."

"Wanna grab a quick breakfast?" Alex asks as we approach the P Street Bridge at the end of our run.

"Sure."

Over breakfast, Alex tells me that her younger sister Walker is flying in from Denver the next day. "She's coming to DC for a friend's wedding. The wedding is not until Saturday, but she's flying in a few days early so that we can spend some time together."

"Oh, yeah. I remember you mentioning that she was coming to town."

"I'm really excited to see her," Alex continues. "I mean, we talk on the phone all the time, but I haven't seen her since Robert's funeral. Usually I see her at Christmas, but she didn't come home this year. She and her boyfriend are starting to get serious, and they spent the holidays with his family."

"So, what are you guys going to do while she is here?" I ask.

"If I can manage it, I hope to take a little time off. We'll probably hit a few tourist sites since she's only been to DC a few times, but mostly I think we will hang out, talk, and stuff our faces with good food. Walker is a total foodie…Hey, speaking of which, do you want join us for dinner on Friday night?"

"Yeah, sure, I'd love to. It would be great to meet your sister, and you know I would never turn down a good meal."

Alex laughs, and I sit back in my chair and try to absorb the fact that she's back in my life. Things feel a little different between us—in a good way. Before, the secret of my past weighed so heavily on my shoulders. I think somehow Alex sensed I wasn't giving her my whole self. Now that the air is clear, things feel easier between us and it feels wonderful.

* * *

I make my way over to Hemlock later that morning, and everyone greets me just as they would on a typical day. I have no idea how or even if Alex explained my absence to people at the office, so I just assume everyone thinks I was on vacation or something.

I make my way to my desk and everything seems pretty much the way I left it. I fire up my computer and start to sort through various files. From what I can tell, no one has been keeping much of an eye on the finances while I've been gone. I roll up my sleeves and get to work. I see Alex sporadically throughout the day, but she's running around like a chicken with its head cut off so she can squeeze in some time off to spend with her sister.

CHAPTER TWENTY-NINE

I work at Hemlock the rest of the week and do my best to get everything up to date. Alex and I manage to get together for lunch one day, but otherwise, she's mostly out of the office at work sites. She gives me a call Friday afternoon.

"Hey Mattie. You holding down the fort at the office?"

"Yeah, everything is under control," I assure her.

"You still up for dinner with me and Walker tonight?" she asks.

"Yeah, of course," I respond enthusiastically.

"Okay, cool. I made reservations at a Vietnamese place in Adams Morgan, but why don't you swing by my place for a quick drink before dinner? Say six o'clock-ish. Then the three of us can walk up to the restaurant together. Does that work?"

"Yeah, that sounds perfect. How's Walker's visit been so far?"

"Oh, God, we've done nothing but talk since she landed. It's really awesome to have her here," she says.

"Good, I'm glad you guys are having a good time. I'm really psyched to meet her."

"She's looking forward to meeting you too. I've told her all about you…Well, not everything…"

"I get it," I say with a laugh. "See you tonight."

We end the call, and I turn back to my computer to finish up one last report before the end of the day.

After work, I head over the Alex's place. I'm nervous for some reason. The significance of the fact that Alex wants me to meet her sister has not escaped me. It's an indication that Alex still considers me as an important part of her life. And, hopefully, as someone who will be part of her life for the foreseeable future.

A woman who looks strikingly like Alex, minus the incredible green eyes, answers the door when I knock.

"Hi, you must be Alex," she says.

"Yep. And you must be Walker," I say and reach out to shake her hand.

"Alex is just finishing getting ready. She should be out in a minute. Can I get you a glass of wine?" Walker asks.

"Yeah, sure. That would be great. Thanks."

"So, Alex tells me you've been helping her out at Hemlock," Walker says as she hands me a glass of wine.

"Yeah, I've been doing a little accounting work for the firm."

"A little accounting work, huh? More like you've totally overhauled our financial system." Alex beams as she enters the room.

I can't help but blush.

Alex walks over and gives me a quick kiss. "I see you two have met?"

The three of us sit out on Alex's balcony and enjoy a glass of wine before it's time to walk up to Adams Morgan. I like Walker instantly. She shares Alex's warmth and awesome sense of humor.

The restaurant is crazy busy given that it's a Friday night, but we luck out and get seated at a table right by the window. It's amazing to see the diversity of people streaming up Eighteenth Street to all the bars and restaurants in Adams Morgan. The three of us quickly bond over the fabulous people watching. Walker excuses herself to go to the bathroom after we place our orders. When she's gone, I reach over and take Alex's hand in mine. "Can I cook dinner for you tomorrow night?"

"Sure. Walker will be at the wedding for most of the evening so, yeah, that would be really nice," she says as she gently caresses my hand.

"Great!" I say just as Walker returns to the table. I instinctively pull my hand away from Alex's.

"Don't worry, Mattie, Alex already told me that she's crazy about you," Walker says with a laugh as she sits back down at the table.

Alex gives me a sheepish look that causes butterflies to dance in my stomach. I can't believe this amazing woman wants to be with me, I think to myself.

Over the course of dinner, I learn some more about the Holland family. It sounds like all four of the Holland sisters played every sport under the sun and they were fiercely competitive with one another. Alex and her two middle sisters were all in high school at the same time and played on the school soccer team together.

"The coach would say, 'Holland, get in the game!' and we would look at him and ask, 'Which one?'" Alex says with a laugh. "I honestly don't think he knew the answer. He would just point to whomever was closest."

"Skiing was the sport the family loved best though," Walker explains. "It was the one thing we could all do together. In the winter, we skied almost every weekend when we were little."

"I remember those ski weekends fondly," Alex says. "Except we always seemed to get our boots and skies mixed, and I remember sometimes wearing boots that were way too small for me," she says with a laugh.

Listening to Alex and Walker makes me a little wistful. It makes me wish my parents were still around or that at least I was on speaking terms with my sister.

By the end of the evening, Walker has convinced Alex and me to come out to Colorado the following winter to try backcountry skiing with her and her boyfriend, Zach. "Zach is director of the avalanche center, so he really knows his stuff and he doesn't mess around," she assures us as we join the throngs of people on the street. I hug them both good-bye before heading back to my apartment.

* * *

I wake up Saturday morning and immediately start to pore over a few cooking websites to figure out what to make Alex for dinner that evening. Since she was a little adventurous last time she made dinner for me, I want to try to do the same for her. Eventually, I pick a recipe for grilled Portobello mushrooms with goat cheese and saffron fettuccine with a bunch of different kinds of tomatoes.

I make a list of what I need and then, in an effort to beat the Saturday crowds, walk over to the "Social Safeway" right after I finish breakfast. When I'm done there, I stop in a little neighborhood wine shop on my way home, and the salesman helps me select a nice bottle of wine to go with what I am cooking.

I get home, unpack the groceries and spend a good portion of the afternoon cooking. Before I know it, it is almost six o'clock and I barely have time to tidy up my apartment and take a quick shower before Alex is due to arrive at seven.

She arrives right on time, and I buzz her up to my place. Alex steps into my apartment and gives me a quick kiss hello. "Smells great, Mattie," she says as I take her coat.

I pour us each a glass of wine, and Alex sits at my kitchen island while I finish making dinner. The only problem is that my attempt at adventurous cooking doesn't go quite as well as I'd hoped. The fettuccine comes out okay, but I totally overcook the Portobello mushrooms and they disintegrate when I try to top them with the goat cheese. It's nearly nine o'clock before we sit down to eat. Alex is gracious when she tries her first bite of the mushrooms. "This is good, Mattie."

I dig in and try a bite. "I'd call it edible, but calling it good might be a serious stretch!" I say with a laugh.

We both manage to clear most of our plates, and Alex mentions that she's supposed to dog sit for her friend Allison in Annapolis the following weekend. "I'd love it if you come and spend the weekend with me in Annapolis. Allison has this really cute house right on the water, and her dog is a big old sweetie."

"Wow, yeah, that sounds fantastic. I'd love to come. Believe it or not, I've never been to Annapolis, plus it would be really nice to spend the weekend with you." I give her a wink.

"Okay, then it's a plan. Why don't we try and leave for Annapolis right after work next Friday?"

"Works for me!" I say as I get up and start to clear the dishes.

Alex gets up to help me clean up the kitchen, but I hold up my hand to stop her. Not only was my meal barely edible, it also required the use of nearly every dish in the apartment and my kitchen is a total disaster. "I'll deal with the dishes later."

Alex tries to protest, but I won't let her into the kitchen. Instead I pour the last of the wine into our glasses and lead her over to the couch in my small living room. Tony Bennett is singing in the background, and before we have a chance to sit down, Alex takes the wineglass out of my hand and sets both of our glasses down on the coffee table.

"Dance with me, Mattie!" she says as she takes my hand and pulls me into her arms. We start to dance slowly around my living room. "This is nice," I whisper in her ear.

"Mmhm." She gives me small, crooked smile before planting a soft kiss on my lips.

I reach up and run my hands through her hair and tug her into a deeper kiss before drawing back to look up into her eyes. "Being with you makes me happy," I say, and lean my forehead against hers. She pulls me closer and lets out a soft, pleasurable groan. We sway back and forth to the music until Alex's phone starts to vibrate on the kitchen counter.

Alex pulls back and looks up at me apologetically. "That's probably Walker. I told her to text me when she was getting ready to leave the wedding." She goes to check her phone, and I sigh, missing the warmth of her body against mine.

"Yep, that's her. She's headed home," she says as she walks back toward me. "I should probably go. She's got keys to my place, but she flies out tomorrow, so I think it would be nice if I was home when she gets back from the wedding."

"Yeah, I agree. I totally understand." I give her a quick peck on the lips before walking over to retrieve her coat from the front closet.

She slips on her coat and leans over to give me a kiss good-bye. I expect a quick kiss on the lips, but she gently pushes me up against the front door and skillfully slides her tongue into my mouth. My tongue eagerly meets hers and minutes pass before she finally steps back.

"Jesus, Alex," I say breathlessly.

She gives me a wicked smile, reaches for the door handle and heads out the door, leaving me wanting so much more.

CHAPTER THIRTY

Spring is in the air, and as a result, things are even crazier than normal at Hemlock the week after Walker's visit. Before I know it, it's Friday and I'm feeling downright giddy about spending the weekend in Annapolis with Alex. We'd hoped to hit the road midafternoon to avoid the worst of the weekend traffic, but Alex gets stuck at a jobsite and it's almost six o'clock by the time we actually get on the road. Traffic is heavy, and it takes us almost two hours to get to Annapolis. It's well after dark by the time we pull into town, and we make a quick pit stop to pick up some beer and pizza before heading on to Allison's house.

I'm famished, and it is complete and utter torture to smell the wonderful aroma seeping from the warm pizza box as we drive the last few miles to Allison's. The tires of Alex's truck crunch on her gravel driveway as we make our way up to the house. I climb out of the truck, and a very large and very excited golden retriever runs up to greet me.

"Hello handsome," I say as I scratch the area just behind his ears. "You must be Cooper?"

"Yeah, that's him. He's a big guy, but he wouldn't hurt a fly," Alex says as she walks around the truck to join me.

We grab our bags out of the truck and follow Cooper up to the house. Alex feels around for the key that Allison was supposed to leave for us and holds it up triumphantly when she finally finds it tucked behind a downspout. She unlocks the door, and we both step inside behind Cooper. Allison's house is small but extremely open. The décor is what I would call contemporary, and the whole front of the house has big picture windows.

"Those windows look out onto Crab Creek," Alex explains. "Wait until you see the view in the morning."

"I bet it's beautiful."

"Both bedrooms are upstairs. How about we throw our bags in her guest room and then dig into that pizza?"

"Okay, but we better make it quick. I might die if I don't have pizza in my mouth in the next two minutes."

We drop our bags and head back downstairs to the kitchen. Alex pulls some plates out of the cupboard and carries them over to the kitchen table while I go in search of a bottle opener for the beer. We sit down and inhale the entire pizza in less than twenty minutes.

"Guess we were hungry, huh?" Alex says with a laugh.

"Oh my God, that was so fucking good. I swear I could eat like five more pieces." I chuckle just as Cooper trots into the room.

"I guess I should take the old guy outside for his evening walk."

"All right, I'll clean up here and see if I can get a fire going in that big fireplace in the living room."

There is a good bit of firewood and newspaper in the bin next to the fireplace, and I manage to get a decent fire going by the time that Alex gets back with the dog.

"Wow, nice fire!" she says. "I'm going to grab another beer, want one?"

I nod, and she goes into the kitchen to grab us each another beer. While she's in the kitchen, I build a little nest on the floor in front of the fire using a few pillows from the couch and a big wool blanket. Alex gives me a curious look when she walks back in the room, and I motion for her to join me on the floor.

She curls up next to me and affectionately reaches up to run a hand through my hair. "Hey you," she says. "I like the little *love* nest that you've built."

"Oh, yeah?" I lean in to gently brush my lips against hers.

We share a few soft kisses before I slip my tongue into her mouth. We kiss deeply for a long time and the desire that has been simmering between us begins to boil. Alex rolls over on top of me and pulls her sweater up over her head before reaching down to help me out of mine. She unclasps my bra and makes quick work of the buttons on my jeans. I slide out of my pants so I'm now lying naked beneath her. She caresses my breasts, and my nipples harden under her touch. She leans down to tease them with her tongue, and I feel the heat build between my legs. I reach up to release her bra, and she hovers one of her large breasts over my mouth as she slides her hand down into my wetness. I suck hard on her nipple as she strokes my throbbing clit and slowly slips her fingers in and out of me. It doesn't take long before my body begins to shudder and I come hard against her.

I look up at Alex. "How is it that you are still wearing pants?" I work to help her slip them off. I resume sucking on her nipple as I start to slowly run my fingers over the silk of her thong. "So wet," I say as I tease her clit through the fabric before tugging her thong down over her ankles.

I roll over so that I'm now on top of her and move my hand back between her legs. I slide inside of her. Her back begins to arch, and I slide down her body to taste her for the first time. She finally lets out a loud moan of release, and I crawl up into her arms. She places small kisses on my head, but neither of us speaks. Both satiated, we eventually doze off in front of the fire.

A full bladder wakes me a few hours later, and I help Alex up to bed. She doesn't fully wake up, but as soon as I climb into bed next to her, she curls up next to me, and I fall asleep relishing the feel of her warm body next to mine.

* * *

The sun wakes us up early Saturday morning, and we decide to take a quick run with the dog before breakfast. As we are walking back up to the house, Alex turns to me. "God, what a beautiful day, huh? This might sound like a crazy idea, but you want to go for sail? Allison said it was okay if we want to use her boat."

"Wow, yeah, that would be awesome. I mean, assuming that you know how to sail?" I laugh. "I took sailing at summer camp, but it would be a major stretch to call me a sailor."

"Yeah, I've done a fair amount of it since I moved to DC. I didn't sail much growing up in Denver, but I've gone out with Allison a million times and she's taught me a lot."

We make a quick run to the grocery store to grab some food for a picnic lunch and dinner that night. I make sandwiches and pack some snacks to take on the boat while Alex gathers up the required sailing gear from Allison's garage.

We wander down toward the water until we reach the U-shaped dock that juts out from Allison's property. The sailboat is on a mooring ball about fifty yards from the dock. The dock is two levels, and the upper deck shelters the slip of water between the "U" formed by the lower dock. There's a small Zodiac rubber dinghy tied up in the slip, and Alex and I climb into that and row out to the sailboat. The Zodiac has a small five-horsepower outboard engine, but given the short distance to the boat, it's just as easy to row. We tie the Zodiac to the back of the sailboat and climb aboard. I stow our picnic basket, cooler, a small blanket, some extra sweaters, and two rain slickers in the small cabin of the boat and then climb up on deck to help Alex rig the boat. It's a beautiful warm day, but Alex insisted that we bring some extra layers of clothing because the weather in the Chesapeake Bay is unpredictable and can change suddenly.

We sail for almost two hours before Alex expertly guides the boat into small a cove next to a sandy spit of land. She gives me the cue to climb up on the bow of the boat as she turns the boat into the wind so that we can lower the sails. There are no other boats within eyesight. It's an absolutely glorious day but is still extremely early in the sailing season. Allison is one of the few people along Crab Creek who even has their boat in the water.

We plan to anchor the boat in the cove and take the Zodiac to shore for lunch, so once the sails are down, I start to prepare the anchor. Once I've got it ready, I look back at Alex and give her thumbs-up and she gives me the cue to toss it overboard and into the water. The cove is only about fifteen feet deep, and the anchor quickly catches on the sandy bottom. I wait for the boat to drift a little bit so that there's a little slack in the anchor line before kneeling down to tie it off. Alex appears on the deck next to me and reaches out a hand to help me to my feet. She pulls me into a quick hug. "Great job, mate."

"Nice job yourself, Captain!"

"You like this little cove?" She gives me a quick peck on the lips.

I look up at her with an approving smile. "It's a beautiful spot, and I can't believe we have it all to ourselves."

"Shall we head to shore for lunch?" She takes my hand and leads me back down toward the Zodiac.

I grab the picnic basket, the cooler, and the blanket, and we both climb in the rubber Zodiac to head toward shore. We had to anchor a good distance from shore because the water quickly gets very shallow around the sand beach and the sailboat draws nearly six feet. Rather than row all the way to shore, Alex fires up the little engine on the Zodiac. As we approach the beach, she kills the engine and pulls it up out of the water so that the Zodiac can coast up onto shore.

"Nicely done, Miss Holland," I say as the Zodiac glides onto the sand. We unload the boat and pull it up higher onto the sand so that it won't float away while we picnic. I pick up the picnic basket and Alex grabs the blanket and small cooler, and we walk toward the small, sandy point.

"How's this?" she asks when we reach the point.

"Perfect," I reply, and she spreads the blanket out on the ground.

We both sit down, and I pull our sandwiches out of the picnic basket and grab us each a sparkling water and some carrot sticks from the cooler.

"The sun feels amazing," I say as I take a big bite of my sandwich.

"Yeah, I can't believe how lucky we got to get a day like this. I looked at the weather before we left the house, and it looks like it will be back to crappy gray spring weather tomorrow."

We eat the rest of lunch in silence and stare out at the sun dancing on the water. When Alex is done eating, she polishes off her water and lies back on the blanket with a sigh. I look down at her, and she tugs at my coat. "Come here, you."

I eagerly comply and rest my head on her chest. It doesn't take long for us both to doze off, and the sun is much lower in the sky when Alex nudges me awake. "It's getting late, we should get back to the sailboat."

I let out a whimper of protest when she rolls her warm body away from mine and stands up. She gives me an understanding look and leans down to pull me up. We gather our stuff and walk back to the beached zodiac.

The wind has died significantly since we arrived, and reluctantly Alex decides that we should motor back to Allison's house rather than sail. The sun is going down quickly, and the temperature is beginning to drop so, as much as I miss the silence of sailing, I know it's the right call.

We get back to the house in under and hour, take a nice hot shower together and get started on dinner.

"What do you think about eating in front of the fire tonight?" Alex suggests.

"That sounds wonderful...I have very fond memories of that fire," I tease, and she playfully snaps a dishtowel on my ass. "I'll go and try and get a fire started."

We watch a movie after dinner before heading up to bed. Once upstairs, we undress one another slowly and climb into bed. The raw desire from the night before is gone, and we take our time exploring each other's bodies and tenderly make love before falling asleep in a tangle of limbs.

I wake up early the next morning. Alex is still sound asleep. She looks so peaceful and I can't bear to wake her, so I quietly slip out of bed, get dressed and take the dog out for a quick walk. As the weather report predicted, it's a gross, rainy day, and neither the dog nor I is too interested in a long walk. He does his business quickly, and we head back to the house. I grab the *New York Times* off the doorstep, towel off the dog and wander into the kitchen to make some coffee.

Alex appears in the kitchen wearing a Vail T-shirt and flannel pajama bottoms as soon as the coffee starts brewing. I can't help but notice that she's not wearing a bra, and I feel a small twinge in my groin as her breasts bob under her shirt when she walks over to pour herself a cup of coffee. We sip our coffee and read the paper before cooking up some bacon and eggs for breakfast. Alex's phone rings just as we finish eating, and she gets up to walk into the front hall where she left her phone. I figure I might as well start the dishes while she's on the phone, so I gather them up and fill the sink with soapy water.

I'm almost done when Alex walks back into kitchen. "It was Allison checking in to make sure we haven't burned down the house and let the dog run away. I assured her that everything is under control…although I chose not to mention the fact that we had sex in her living room."

"I think that was probably wise." I chuckle.

Alex walks up behind me as I set the last dish in the drying rack. She presses up against my back, wraps her arms around my waist and starts to nibble at my neck. "Thanks for doing the dishes," she says between nibbles, and then slides her hands up and begins to caress my breasts through my sweater.

I let out a little squeal of surprise and feel my nipples harden as she teases them with her thumbs. She turns me around to face her and leans in for a slow but deep kiss, pausing briefly to reach down and pull my sweater up over my head and masterfully unhook my bra. She plants a kiss on each of my breasts before reaching down to quickly pull her T-shirt up over her head to reveal two swollen breasts. I cannot resist the urge to reach up and run my fingers over her taut nipples.

Alex pulls me into another deep kiss, and the sensation of our bare breasts rubbing together as we kiss puts my groin in overdrive. I push her back against the kitchen island as our tongues continue to lash together. We're both panting when Alex eventually breaks the kiss to look at me with hooded eyes. "We better hightail it up to the bedroom before I take you right here on the kitchen island...Allison might prefer that we not have sex in every room of her house!" she says with a laugh.

I grab for her hand, and we practically run back upstairs to the bedroom.

When we get upstairs she kicks off her flannel pajama bottoms, gently pushes me down on the bed and works to unbutton my jeans and slide them off my body. She takes one of my nipples in her mouth as she moves her hand down between my legs. Alex quickly brings me close to the edge as she slides her fingers back and forth through my wetness. My entire body is on fire as she moves down to take my throbbing clit in her mouth. It takes only a few swipes of her tongue to push me over the cliff.

Still breathing deeply, I roll over on top of her and slide my hand deep inside of her. She is incredibly wet and comes almost instantly. I roll over onto my back, and she curls up next to me. I can hear the rain dancing on the roof as we both doze off.

We finally emerge from the bedroom late morning and decide to take the dog for a walk in the park. The day is still gloomy, but the rain has mostly stopped and the dog needs some exercise. It's late afternoon by the time we get back from the park, and we reluctantly pack our bags and tidy the house before driving back to DC. Allison should be home around dinnertime, so the dog should be fine on his own until she gets back.

CHAPTER THIRTY-ONE

Alex and I make a feeble attempt to keep our relationship under wraps at the office, but before long, the entire office knows about the two of us and we give up the charade. Apparently, the tender smiles and longing glances that pass between us were a dead giveaway. At first, I was a little worried that some of the employees would be uncomfortable with the fact that Alex and I were dating but, from what I can tell, everyone seems genuinely happy that Alex is in a relationship with someone.

"Are you okay that we've been outed at the office?" I ask her one evening.

"Yeah. I mean, I was a little worried at first. Most of the people at the firm have been around for a while and they knew Robert well. I wasn't sure how they'd react especially since you're, um, a woman but everyone has been really supportive."

"Okay, good. I just wanted to make sure."

"After Robert died I started working even longer hours than normal. Partly because I was now doing the work of two people but also because it was my way of coping, or maybe, not coping, with the fact that he was gone. I think people at the office are happy that I'm now leaving at a reasonable hour on occasion. I have you to thank for that," she says and gives me a long smile.

* * *

My birthday is in late April, and Alex surprises me with a weekend trip to the Inn at Little Washington. The Inn is located in northern Virginia about two hours west of DC, and I've always wanted to go there. Not only is it an incredibly romantic historic inn, but it also happens to have a Michelin-starred restaurant at which all overnight guests are guaranteed a reservation. I know scoring a room there is no easy feat, so I can't believe Alex was able to get us in.

My actual birthday falls on a Thursday this year, so Alex makes me flank steak and grilled asparagus on her grill. We agreed to a quiet dinner at home on the actual day since we're leaving for the Inn the next day. On Friday, we somehow manage to sneak out of the office around three o'clock so that we can hit the road before the peak of rush-hour traffic. Traffic out of the city is still pretty heavy, but we still make it to the Inn a little after six o'clock.

We drive into the Colonial village where the Inn is located and park Alex's truck in a small gravel lot outside the Inn's main building.

A very tall, thin, twenty-something woman greets us as we approach the reception desk. "Hello, and welcome to the Inn at Little Washington. May I have your name, please?" she says a little too pleasantly.

"Um, yes, the reservation is under Alaska Holland," Alex replies as she digs in her purse for her wallet.

"Alaska, that's a very unusual name. I like it," the woman says as she starts to peck at her computer. "I see you are staying with us for two nights. We have you in a beautiful room in The Parsonage, the Victorian house just across the street from the main Inn. You'll love it, the rooms were just renovated this past year," she says as she hands Alex a registration card to complete before continuing. "You're all set for dinner at the Inn's restaurant tomorrow night...and let's see, it looks like you've arranged for private dining this evening. A table will be set for you in our library and, as you requested, be available for you at eight o'clock." she says as she looks up at Alex to confirm that everything she's said is correct.

"Yes, that all sounds right," Alex says to the tall woman before giving me a little wink.

"Do you need any assistance with your luggage?" the receptionist asks as she hands Alex two room keys.

"No thank you, we don't have much. I think we can manage on our own," Alex replies, and we turn to head back out to the parking lot.

As soon as we're outside, I turn to Alex. "Private dining in the library? Like bringing me here wasn't enough? You sure know how to sweep a woman off her feet!" I wrap my arm across her shoulders as we walk back to the truck.

We move her truck across the street near the Parsonage, grab our bags and head off in search of our room. We find it on the second floor, and Alex slides one of the keys into the lock.

"Wow!" Alex says as she steps inside the room and takes a look around.

"Holy shit," I echo when I step in behind her.

The room is fairly large and exquisitely decorated—it's less ornate than the décor of the main inn, which suits me just fine—with furniture that somehow manages to look contemporary and English country at the same time. A fire has been set in the wood-burning fireplace, and French doors open to a balcony that overlooks the meticulously maintained gardens, which are bursting with color.

Alex steps out onto the balcony to take in the view. "I could seriously get used to this! When I made the reservation, the person explained that Parsonage offers a more modern take on the Inn's English country house aesthetic, whatever that means." Alex says as she steps back into the room.

We quickly unpack, and start to freshen up for dinner. We're in the process of changing into our clothes for dinner when there's a knock at the door and a deep voice says, "Room service." Alex and I are both half naked, and we stare at each, not sure what to do. I grab a robe out of the closet, and Alex ducks into the bathroom.

"Coming," I say as I tie the robe and head for the door. I open the door to find a well-dressed man with a bottle of champagne nestled in a bucket of ice and two champagne flutes. I let him in the room, and he sets the champagne and glasses on a table near the French doors before politely excusing himself.

Alex emerges from the bathroom. "Wow! Where did that come from?"

I notice that there is a little card tucked under the bucket of ice. I pick it up and open it. "Oh my gosh, it's from Ellen for my birthday. I mentioned to her that you were bringing me here… How sweet."

"I'll say. What do you say we pop that bad boy open and enjoy some champagne before dinner?" she asks.

We finish getting dressed, and I settle into one of the chairs on our balcony while Alex opens the champagne. I hear a pop, and she steps out on the balcony with two flutes of champagne a moment later.

I take one and raise it in the air. "I would like to make a toast…to the crazy-ass biker that almost took you out in Rock Creek Park. If it wasn't for him, I may never have met you!"

"I'll toast to that!" Alex says as we clink our glasses together.

We sit on the balcony, sip champagne and soak in our beautiful surroundings. Alex tops off both of our glasses before we make our way to dinner.

The very tall woman at the front desk greets us warmly when we step back inside the main inn. "Back for dinner?" she asks.

"Yes, we are," Alex replies.

"Let me show you to the library."

We follow her across a large living room to a set of French doors. She opens the doors to reveal possibly the most inviting space I have ever seen. The walls are lined with books, and there's a fire crackling in the fireplace. The bookshelves are softly lit, but otherwise, the only light in the room is coming from the fire and a handful of candles that adorn the small dinner table set in the middle of the room.

The waiter pulls out a chair for each of us and presents us each with a handwritten menu. He points to the menus and explains that we will be enjoying their "petite" tasting menu. Petite because it only includes five small plates and dessert rather than twelve courses served in the main restaurant. The menu for the evening includes wine pairings, so there is no need for us to order a bottle of wine.

As soon as the waiter leaves the room, I reach across the table for Alex's hand. "It doesn't get much more romantic than this. Thank you for all of this, Alex. This will, without a doubt, be the most amazing birthday that I have ever had," I say, and I really mean it. Spending my birthday at the Inn at Little Washington is an incredible treat, but spending it with Alex is what really matters. This is the first birthday that I've spent with someone I…someone I *love*, I think to myself as I swallow hard and look up into her sparkling green eyes.

"You're welcome." She gives me a tender smile.

I consider telling her right then… Telling her what I just realized myself—that I love her…that I am in love with her. But I cannot find my voice, so I just let out a small sigh. We sit in silence, just appreciating the moment and relishing our surroundings until the waiter reappears a few moments later with our first dish and wine pairing.

We linger over crisp endive and tangy pear salad, lamb Carpaccio, mouthwatering spinach pasta with truffles, tender short ribs, and moist sea bass before finishing off with a pungent cheese plate for dessert.

"That was truly one of the best meals I've ever had in my life! I cannot imagine how they can top that tomorrow night," I say as I savor the last bite of cheese.

"Yeah, that was *unbelievable*." Alex licks her lips slowly and then dabs them with her napkin. "I mean, I know this place is supposed to having amazing food, but I'm still blown away by how good it was." The waiter returns to see if he can bring us any tea, coffee, or espresso. We both decline but gush over the meal we have just enjoyed.

After he leaves, Alex and I wander back over to the Parsonage. Once we get back in the room, Alex gives me a mischievous look. "Did you see that awesome Jacuzzi tub in the bathroom? What do you say we test it out?"

"If it means getting naked with you, count me in!"

I follow Alex into the bathroom. She turns on the water to fill the tub and adds a few dashes of the Inn's bath salts. While the tub fills, we strip out of our dinner clothes, toss them over the back of a chair and then slip into the warm bubbling water. Alex lies back against the end of the tub, and I nestle myself between her legs and lean back against her breasts. She wraps her arms around me, and I lean back to rest my head on her shoulder.

"This is heaven," I whisper, and let out a contented sigh.

"Uh-huh." Alex nibbles playfully on my ear before reaching up to grab the bar of soap off the ledge of the tub. She runs the soap over my arms and shoulders and gently lathers up one breast and then the other. The sensation causes me to squirm a little bit, and my nipples stand to full attention. When she's done, I confiscate the soap and ungracefully flop around in the water as I try to reposition myself so that we're facing each other. I maneuver my legs around her torso and begin to run the soap in slow circles over her large breasts.

Alex looks up at me, and her incredible green eyes are full of desire. "Out of the tub now," she commands.

I splash some water on her breasts to rinse away the soap and work to extract myself from the tub. "Your wish is my command, Madame," I say flirtatiously as I step on the floor mat and reach for the two plush hotel robes hanging on the back of the bathroom door. Alex climbs out of the tub after me, and I hand her one of the robes. She ties her robe and takes my hand to lead me back into the bedroom.

She drops my hand when we reach the side of the bed and quickly runs over to pull the curtain across the French doors. "I'd rather not have the whole hotel watch as I ravage your body," she says with a wicked grin as she walks back toward the bed.

"Oh, really, ravage, huh?" I ask playfully.

She doesn't answer but reaches down to untie my robe and push it open to expose my naked body. She lets out what sounds almost like a growl as she reaches out to touch one of my very erect breasts and then leans down to take my nipple in her mouth. Alex sucks hard on one nipple and then moves to the other before pushing me down on the bed.

She slips out of her robe and crawls on top of me. She slides her tongue into my mouth while simultaneously slipping her hand between my legs. "Oh, so nice and wet," she says huskily as she slowly slides her fingers inside of me and then over my throbbing clit.

She slides her hand back inside me, and I begin to move with her. I reach up to kiss her as I begin to tense against her hand, and I let out a very loud moan before collapsing back on the bed. "That was amazing, Alex," I mutter as I try to catch my breath. "It's been a long time since someone made me come that hard…"

Alex looks down at me and gives me a big grin. "Glad I could be of service," she says with a chuckle.

In a quick move, I reach up and grab her shoulders and roll over on top of her so that I can return the favor.

* * *

The next morning, we head down and have breakfast in the small dining room located on the first floor of the Parsonage. It's an incredibly beautiful sunny day, and after breakfast, we plan to set out on a short day-hike in the nearby Blue Ridge Mountains.

As we finish eating, our waiter brings out the two gourmet box lunches we'd requested. I tuck them into my daypack next to the water bottles I filled up before we left the room. Alex, always the Girl Scout, has filled her pack with two spare fleece jackets, two raincoats, a flashlight, a bag of gorp (aka trail mix,) and some other odds and ends, and I kiddingly remind her that we are just doing a short hike, not climbing Mt. Kilimanjaro.

"It's good to be prepared," she replies defensively and punches me playfully in the arm as we walk out to her truck.

The trail that we've picked is about thirty minutes from the inn. After we park the car at the trailhead, we change into our hiking boots and set off into the woods. The hiking trail starts off following a river and is basically flat for the first hour, but then the slope increases and the last mile is pretty much straight uphill. We're both breathing pretty hard when we finally reach the rocky summit and pause to take in the breathtaking views of the valley below and nearby mountains. We scramble over the rocks until we find a sundrenched perch nestled between the rocks and kick back to soak in the view.

"Well, I guess the hellacious climb was worth it, huh?" Alex asks as she leans down to loosen the laces on her boots.

"Yeah, it's beautiful up here," I reply. "How about some lunch? I'm starving!" I reach to pull the box lunches out of my pack. I set the lunches out on the rocks in front of us, pop open the lids and peek inside. "Yum," I say as I pull a mozzarella, tomato, and basil sandwich out of my box and dig my teeth into the homemade bread.

"Yeah, damn, this is pretty decadent for a hike," Alex says after she finishes chewing her first big bite. "I'm usually happy if I have a peanut butter sandwich."

Our lunches also include a small container of mixed berries, and we feed them playfully to one another, not even noticing that an older couple has joined us on the peak. We wave hello to them sheepishly as we finish up our meal.

Before long, two more groups of hikers reach the summit. "Wow, our timing was really good," I say to Alex.

"Yeah, I can't believe we got the summit to ourselves while we ate lunch," Alex replies.

"Knowing the Inn, they probably arranged it!" I say with a laugh.

"It would not surprise me."

"Think they offer room service up here? A beer would taste really good right now."

"In your dreams, Pearson," Alex says as she stands and pulls on her backpack. I follow suit, and we begin our way back down.

CHAPTER THIRTY-TWO

That night, we feast on dinner in the Inn's biggest draw, their Michelin-rated restaurant. The main restaurant offers three different tasting menus, and Alex and I both opt for the vegetarian menu since we'd had a lot of meat and fish the night before. The waiter inquires whether we are interested in adding the wine pairings, and we nod in unison. Over the next three hours, we savor every bite of the dozen or so mouthwatering dishes that appear from the kitchen, each one with its own unique flavor and each beautifully presented. Like the previous evening, each dish is just a small taste, but I feel very satisfied when the waiter brings out our dessert.

After dinner, Alex and I decide to take a short stroll in the lush gardens surrounding the inn. The moon is nearly full, and although the sun has long since set, the air is still relatively warm. We walk hand in hand, and Alex points out some of the many flowers that are just starting to bloom. Even though I've been working at Hemlock for a few months now, I still don't really know a thing about flowers, and I enjoy listening to her explain the varieties.

We pause when we reach the far side of the garden where there's a small pond with a gurgling fountain. The pond is lit up, and you can see koi swimming around in the shadows.

Alex reaches up to brush her hand over my cheek and gives me a soft smile. "You look beautiful in the moonlight, Mattie." She leans in to kiss me softly on the lips. She pulls back and stares into my eyes while taking my hands in hers. "Mattie," she almost whispers. "I think I've gone and fallen in love you."

"Oh, Alex…" I lean my forehead against hers and let out a shaky breath. "I've gone and fallen in love with you too." I give her a quick kiss before continuing. "God knows, I wasn't looking for it, but you came out of nowhere and swept me off of my feet." She wraps her arms around me, and we slowly sway back and forth. "What do you say we head back to the room?" I finally ask, my voice raspy with emotion.

We barely make it inside our room before we rip each other's clothes off and start devouring each other's bodies. Before long, Alex has me down on the coffee table with her head between my legs. She strokes my clit with her tongue and slides her fingers inside me. I rock back and forth gently and let the pleasure build until an orgasm thrusts through me.

I roll off the coffee table and chase Alex over toward the couch. She has her back to me, and I reach around to take one of her bare breasts in my hand. I squeeze her breast tightly and push her down toward the couch so that I can enter her from behind with my other hand. I knead her nipple while she rides my hand, finally moaning loudly as she comes against my hand.

"Jesus, our poor neighbors." She laughs as she turns to face me.

I give her a quick kiss. "Yeah, especially because I am not done with you yet," I say as I squat down to place my mouth between her legs.

We have sex in various positions throughout the room until we eventually fall exhausted and satiated into bed.

I sleep like a brick until a soft knock on our door wakes us promptly at nine o'clock. I crawl out of bed, slip into a robe and quickly gather some of our clothes off the floor before answering the door. It's a waiter with the room service breakfast we'd ordered the evening before, and I direct him to roll the table over near the couch.

Once he's gone, Alex climbs out of bed and pads to the bathroom. "Damn, I'm sore," she says when she emerges from the bathroom. "I'm not sure if it's from that killer hike or our after-dinner gymnastics." She snickers.

"Probably a combination of both." I laugh as I pull the tops off the various steaming plates that have just been delivered.

Check-out time is not until noon, so we leisurely sip coffee and nibble on our omelets while we flip through the Sunday *Washington Post* and occasionally share knowing glances.

CHAPTER THIRTY-THREE

A couple of weeks after our trip to the Inn at Little Washington, Alex and her lead designer Paul head off to Seattle for a few days to attend some landscaping conference. I spend most of the time Alex is gone working at Hemlock. I stay late at the office nearly every night, and tonight is no different. My back aches from hunching over the computer all day, and I finally decide to call it quits and head back to my apartment on Q Street.

As soon as I step foot onto the sidewalk, I'm struck at how busy the streets are for a weeknight. I rack my brain for the reason, and it finally occurs to me that it's Cinco de Mayo. DC always did celebrate Cinco de Mayo in style with everything from pub crawls to parades, and that would explain why so many festive people are wandering the streets.

I cannot believe that it's already May. As I continue to walk home, I decide it's time for me to take a trip to Vermont. I really want to pay a visit to my farm. I stashed almost all my share of the cash from the heists in an old deer stand on my land, and I want to go get it before someone else finds it. It would also be good to check in with Todd and, if time permits, grab a few of my personal belongings from my sublet in Burlington.

I decide to give Todd a call when I get home to tell him I'm considering a visit to Vermont.

"Do you think I'm crazy?" I ask.

"Nah, I mean, you shouldn't advertise your visit or anything, but it's been complete radio silence as far as the police are concerned. I think the last time I heard anything from them was February," he says.

"All right, well, that's encouraging," I reply.

"I don't think you're totally out of the woods yet, Mattie, but I'm definitely off their radar, and I think that bodes well for you too."

"Well, that settles it. I'm coming."

"How are you going to get here?" he asks.

"I'll probably take the train," I answer. Amtrak runs a daily train between DC and Vermont that is aptly called the Vermonter.

"You're welcome to use Kat's old Subaru station wagon when you're here. I just haven't had the heart to sell it yet."

"Thanks, Todd. That's very kind of you. I want to try and come up next weekend, but I'll drop you a line when I know for sure," I reply.

* * *

Over dinner the next night, I tell Alex that I'm thinking about heading up to Vermont the following weekend, and she insists on coming along even though it's high season for Hemlock. "There is no way you are going without me!" she protests as she gets up to help herself to seconds of the delicious polenta with grilled vegetables she managed to whip together after work. "Plus, how are you going to get there?"

I explain my plan to take the train and then drive Kat's car once I get to Vermont.

"How long will it take by train?"

"Well, the train makes a lot of stops between DC and Vermont, so the entire journey takes more than twelve hours each way…but, unlike flying, you can get up and walk around a train."

"Why don't we take my truck?"

Eventually, I agree that driving makes sense, and honestly, I think I'm somewhat relieved not to have to drive Kat's car around. Plus, I admit, it would be nice to have Alex along with me for what is likely to be an emotional trip.

It will take us at least nine hours to get to Vermont if we drive, and we'll go right by New York City, so I propose that we stop there on the way up and have dinner with Ellen and Andy and Sandy. I really want Alex to meet them, and it will help break up the drive.

After dinner, I do the dishes and Alex heads to her study to catch up on some emails. When I'm done, I poke my head into her study. "Hey, I am going to give Todd and Ellen a call to confirm the dates with them."

"Cool. I'm really excited to meet them. This is going to be a little adventure!" she says, and gives me a wink.

I head back out to the kitchen and call Ellen and Todd.

As Alex and I are getting ready for bed later that night, I give her a quick update on the travel plans for Vermont. "I talked to both Todd and Ellen tonight," I say as I look for the toothpaste in the medicine cabinet.

"Oh, good. Are they both around this weekend?" Alex asks as she spreads some sort of wrinkle-be-gone potion on her face.

"Yep, they'll both be around. The plan is for us to stay with Ellen in New York on Friday night. She's going to check with Andy and Sandy and see if they can join us for dinner." I pause briefly to put toothpaste on my toothbrush. "Then we'll meet up with Todd for dinner in Vermont on Sunday. Does that all sound okay?"

"Yep, it all sounds good to me. Will we head back to DC on Monday?"

"Yesh, wowl dwive back fewst ting Mowday mawning," I say with a mouthful of toothpaste. I rinse my mouth and try again. "Yes, we'll drive back first thing Monday morning."

CHAPTER THIRTY-FOUR

Alex and I hit the road right after lunch the following Friday to make our way to New York. Traffic is surprisingly light for a Friday, and we get into the city a little after five o'clock. We circle the block near Ellen's apartment and manage to find a legal parking spot on the street a few blocks away. We gather our luggage out of the back of the truck and walk down the street toward Ellen's apartment building.

The doorman greets us as we walk in the lobby. "Good evening. How may I help you ladies?"

"Good evening. We are here to see Ellen Church," I reply, and he reaches for the phone to call up to her apartment.

"All set, ladies. Let me show you to the elevator."

Ellen is standing outside her door when we get off the elevator on her floor. She gives me a hug and kiss on the cheek and then turns to Alex. "Mattie has told me *so much* about you, Alex. It's nice to finally meet you."

"*So much*, huh?" Alex grins at me, and I blush.

"Oh, god! You guys have it bad." Ellen laughs and then leads us into her apartment.

Alex and I freshen up and join Ellen in the living room for a glass of wine before we have to go meet Andy and Sandy for dinner. As we sip our wine, Ellen peppers Alex with questions. I know Ellen means well and her questions are generally benign—how long have you been in DC, how long were you married, where did you grow up, where did you go to school—but she's still putting Alex through the wringer. Finally, in an effort to give poor Alex a break, I ask Ellen how things are going on her end.

"Well, Sandy was over here a few weeks ago, and we ran into an old professor that has lived in the building for something like forty-three years. Anyway, Sandy introduced us, and after that, I kept running into him. One day when we ran into each other in the mailroom, he mentioned that he was just returning from his weekly bridge game. So, of course I told him that I was an avid bridge player, and he invited me to join his weekly bridge group." Ellen turns to Alex. "I'm not sure if Mattie told you, but I am a total bridge fanatic. I lived in Manhattan for a while after law school, and my ex-husband and I were in like three bridge groups. Seriously. It's weird—playing bridge always helped relax me because it was one of the few times I could totally block out work.

"Well, to make a long story short," she continues, "the professor and I got to know each other a bit better, and he recently asked me to help him with some legal research for a new book he's working on. So, between playing bridge, the legal work for Andy and Sandy and the book research, I'm keeping pretty busy…which is good."

"That is really great, Ellen!" I say.

"Yeah, it's funny how things work out." She glances at her watch. "We should probably make our way to the East Village to meet Sandy and Andy."

* * *

The next morning, I run out and buy some New York City bagels, and Ellen makes us bacon and eggs before Alex and I jump back in her truck to continue the drive to Vermont.

Once we wind our way out of the city, Alex looks over at me. "So, run me through our nutty Vermont itinerary again."

I give her a sympathetic smile and start to run through all that I hope to pack into our brief trip to Vermont. "Sure! Okay, well, tonight we stay in Burlington. Which reminds me, I need to find us a hotel for the night. Todd invited us to stay with him in Vermont, but I decided that was too risky. I figure I'll just find a room on the Hotels Tonight app. What do you think?"

"Works for me," she replies as she drums the steering wheel softly to the beat of the song on the radio.

I find a pretty sweet deal at the Hilton in downtown Burlington, so I book that. "All right, we're all set with the hotel so we'll stay in Burlington tonight. I figure we can just grab dinner when we get there and hopefully get to bed at a reasonable hour. Then, we can swing by my apartment in Burlington first thing in the morning before we drive out to my farm. The visit to the farm will likely take a few hours, especially since we have to go in the back way. Like we discussed before we left DC, I think it's best that we avoid cruising up my driveway in broad daylight."

I look over at Alex, and she nods in agreement so I continue. "After that, we'll meet Todd at Ellen's house in Stowe for dinner. Ellen's brother is using the house for the weekend, but he will be long gone by dinnertime on Sunday so Ellen suggested we meet Todd for dinner there… and then you and I can also spend the night there. I guess that's about it. We'll head back to DC on Monday. Does that all sound agreeable to you?"

"Sure. It sounds like quite a little escapade, but I am totally up for it!" she says with a chuckle.

We arrive in Burlington after dark, valet the truck at the hotel and head inside to check in. We drop off our bags, and then Alex and I walk along Church Street—a pedestrian marketplace that extends for about ten blocks in the center of town and is completely and permanently closed off to cars. We pop into a few shops, and Alex goes crazy when we come upon an old-fashioned candy store. She fills a bag with a few carefully selected but gross-sounding flavors of jelly beans. Afterward, we sit on a bench outside the store and take turns tossing jelly beans into the air and trying to catch them in our mouth. The jelly beans are in fact pretty disgusting, but I'm laughing so hard I don't care.

We decide to head over to Flatbread and order a take-away pizza. While we wait for it to be prepared, we decide to grab a beer at the bar. The restaurant is buzzing, but I spot two empty stools at the end of bar and start to elbow our way through the crowd.

After surveying the vast selection of beers they have on tap, Alex and I both order a local pale ale called Yard Sale because we like the name—a yard sale is when you take a serious wipeout on the ski slopes and leave your equipment strewn in your wake. I'm only mildly worried that someone will recognize me, but I am sporting a baseball hat and we're in a dark corner of the bar, so I figure I'm probably safe. My biggest fear, of course, is running into Conrad, but he lives way down in Charlotte, and I know he never steps foot in the city on the weekends.

I get a text on my phone just as we're finishing our beer to alert me that our pizza is ready. Alex goes up to get the pizza from the take-away window while I settle the bill with the bartender. While I'm trying to get his attention, I notice that the bar sells one and two-liter growlers (basically a jug of beer), so I order one of those and then head over to find Alex by the front door.

"Look what I got!" I hold up the growler for her to see.

"Sweet, I didn't know they sold those here." She gives me a high five.

We head back to the hotel, inhale our pizza and polish off the growler before climbing into bed to watch a movie.

CHAPTER THIRTY-FIVE

Alex motivates me to get out of bed early the next morning to go for a run along the lakefront before breakfast. I moan and groan at first, but once we start running, I punch her arm softly. "Thanks for getting my sorry ass out of bed!"

"You're welcome. Maybe that growler we had last night was not such a great idea, huh?" she asks with a laugh.

"Yeah, no shit, but it sure was good," I reply as I try to keep up with her pace.

After the run, we take a quick shower and walk over to my sublet.

We make the visit to my apartment very brief. I have no interest in lingering, and I grab my laptop and a few other personal items before we lock up and start to walk back to the hotel.

Alex pauses after we've walked a few blocks. "Do you ever worry that Todd or someone else will turn you in to the police?" she asks.

"No," I answer somewhat confidently. "Todd and Sarah's ex-husband Jake are the only people that have any idea about the full extent of our burglaries. Jake has no idea where I am or how to contact me, and I know Todd would never say anything because, ultimately, he would be implicating Kat and possibly himself. Plus, I trust Todd completely."

I tell her briefly about the fiasco with Conrad and subsequent visit from the police. "Calling him was a huge mistake on my part and almost got me caught," I say. "But, I haven't tripped up again and hopefully, as far as he is concerned, I've disappeared into thin air."

I add, "Before I decided to come to Vermont, I did ask Todd if he's heard from the police recently and he said he hadn't. As far as I know, the police still only know about our involvement at Schuyler House. That puts me and Ellen pretty low on the criminal totem pole." I look over at Alex to make sure I've adequately answered her question.

"That all makes sense, I think," she says as we reach the hotel.

"How about I run up and grab our bags from the room while you check out?" I suggest.

"Good plan. I'll also ask the valet to bring the truck around."

I gather our belongings from the room. By the time I get back downstairs, the valet has already retrieved Alex's truck. We both climb in, and I direct her out of the city and toward my farm, which is located about fifteen miles from downtown Burlington in a small, rural town called Jericho.

We take I-89 to Richmond and then take back roads that start off paved but eventually turn to dirt. My farm is on a dirt road, off a dirt road, and the driveway up to the cabin is nearly a quarter-mile long. Alex slows as we pass my place, but we don't pull in since we've already agreed that it's too risky to just drive up the driveway. Instead, I guide her to a nearby trailhead for the Long Trail—the oldest long-distance trail in the US; it was actually the inspiration for the Appalachian Trail and coincides with it for about one hundred miles.

We park her truck in the small dirt parking area near the trailhead. It's slightly overcast but otherwise a fairly nice day; however, there is only one other car in the lot. I am not that surprised though because it's only May and the trail is likely to be very wet and muddy given that the snow has only recently melted. We both change into hiking boots, load up our daypacks with some supplies and hit the trail.

We hike for about a half mile and then, after checking that no one else is around, cut off the trail and bushwhack for another quarter mile or so until we step foot on the eastern edge of my property. I lead the way to my cabin. When we finally reach it, I go in search of my spare key. I left one of those magnetic Hide-A-Key cases stuck to the underside of an old, rusted wheelbarrow, and I'm able to locate it pretty easily. I extract the key from the case, open the cabin door and lead Alex inside the small space.

"This place is so incredibly cute," Alex says as she looks around the cabin.

"I know, isn't it?" I say with a sigh as my eyes wander over the rustic décor, small open kitchen, wood burning stove and bedroom loft. "I really love this place…I'd always thought that I'd keep the cabin even after I'd built a larger house on the property."

I try to set my emotions aside and focus on the task at hand, but it's hard not think about my old life, the life I had to walk away from. Living in DC has made it easier to push it all to the back of my mind, but now, standing here in my cabin, so many memories come rushing back. I loved it here, and I'd planned to grow old here. Now that future is far from certain. I know I made my bed and I have to sleep in it, but it doesn't mean it's easy.

I sit down on a small stool near the fireplace and try to pull myself together. Alex rubs my back. "You okay?" she asks.

"Yeah. It's just hard," I reply and let out a long sigh. "I'm glad that you got to see the place though," I say and give her a smile.

"Me too, baby."

Eventually, I get up and start to scrounge around for a hammer and screwdriver. Once I find them, I grab a flashlight off the wall, and we head back outside.

"So, where to now?" Alex asks.

"To the deer stand! Follow me, it's not too far." I lead the way toward the more wooded section of my property.

CHAPTER THIRTY-SIX

The deer stand is made of two-by-fours and plywood and has a metal roof. It sits up in a large maple tree about twenty-five feet off the ground and has a wooden ladder that reaches to the ground. I scale the ladder and poke my head inside the stand. The interior is fairly basic and includes only a built-in wooden bench covered with a strip of carpet and a few wooden shelves. I crawl up inside the stand, pull out my hammer and start working to try and loosen a section of the plywood floor. I quickly get one of the boards loose and lift it up to expose a small cavity underneath. I reach for my flashlight and shine it around the cavity until I find what I'm looking for: a moldy blowup camping mat tucked in the back corner. I switch off my flashlight and step into the cavity.

By now, Alex has joined me up in the deer stand, and we work together to pull the mat out of the floor. It's pretty heavy, but finally we manage to drag it up onto the intact part of the floor and spread it out. My hands are filthy, and I wipe them on my pants and push my hair out of my face before grabbing my flashlight again. I turn it on and scan the mat to look for a duct tape patch. When I hid the money up here, I'd cut a hole in the side of the camping mat, slipped the cash inside and then patched the hole back up with duct tape.

Finally, I locate the patch, peel it off and reach my hand deep inside the mat. I feel around and pull out the first bundle of cash that I touch. I continue to pull out bundle after bundle until I can no longer find any more with my hand. Just to be sure, I shine my flashlight around inside the camping mat and, seeing nothing else, toss the mat aside.

I turn my attention to evaluating the massive pile of cash that now covers the floor of the deer stand. I figure that I must have pulled out at least seventy-five bundles of cash—a third of which are comprised of euros and the rest comprised of dollars. I take in a really deep breath and look up at Alex. "Shit, there's a lot more here than I thought…If I had to guess, I'd say there's a few million bucks. What do you think?"

Alex stares back at me with a completely dazed look. "Holy…fucking shit, Mattie…Uh, yeah, that seems like a good guess," she stammers. "I guess I'm just a little stunned by the amount of money. And the fact that it's all in cash is all the more astonishing."

"Well, I hope we can fit in all in our packs!" I say dumbly.

We both seem somewhat paralyzed until I eventually make use of my limbs and begin to divvy up the bundles between our daypacks. Alex snaps out of her paralysis and starts to assist me. It takes some effort, but we manage to stuff all the cash into our packs. I toss the now-empty camping mat back into the cavity and use my hammer to secure the floorboard back into place. Once I'm done, Alex climbs down out of the deer stand, and I toss the two overly stuffed daypacks down to the ground before climbing down after her.

I'm extremely grateful that some of the cash is in euros rather than dollars. If all the cash had been in dollars, I am not sure we could have fit it all in our packs—euros come in higher denominations than dollars, and thus the equivalent amount takes up a lot less space when it's in euros, assuming it is in €500 notes.

The packs are now really heavy, so we help each other slip them on and begin to walk back toward the cabin. I set the tools inside the front door and then close and lock the door. I hide the key back under the wheelbarrow, and we start to bushwhack our way back to the Long Trail. We finally break out of the woods and hit the main trail, and a moment later we run into two older, rather chatty gentlemen.

They eye the large packs that Alex and I both have strapped to our backs. "You gals sure have some big packs! Did you sleep out in the woods last night?" the taller of the two men asks, but he continues talking without giving us a chance to answer. "It sure was a cold one for this time of year," he says as he pokes my pack with his walking stick.

I'm thrown a little off guard but finally respond. "Ah…Nope, we are just training for a big hike so we are carrying a little extra weight to help get in shape." I laugh nervously praying that no cash is sticking out the top of my pack.

"Wow, good for you gals! Enjoy the rest of this beautiful day," the shorter man says, and they both turn to continue up the trail.

As soon as they are out of earshot, Alex turns to me. "Real smooth, Pearson!"

"Ha ha! What did you want me to say? *Oh no, we are just lugging around a few million bucks*." I laugh and slap her playfully on the butt before we start back down the trail.

* * *

It's nearly dark by the time that we get back to the trailhead where we left the truck. The trek to the cabin took longer than I thought, and we are probably going to be late meeting Todd for dinner in Stowe. Once we climb in the truck, I give Todd a quick call to tell him we will be a little late and ask him if we can pick anything up on our way. He says he will take care of dinner but asks if we can stop and pick up some beer.

Alex navigates the truck back down toward Richmond Town Center, and we stop at the small corner market to buy a few six-packs before jumping back onto I-89 toward Stowe.

We get to Ellen's house a little after seven o'clock and we share a laugh when we walk in the door and see a Flatbread pizza box on the kitchen counter.

"What's so funny?" Todd asks as he gives me a hug.

"Just so happens that we had pizza from Flatbread last night…Poor Alex is going to think that's the only food they make in Vermont," I respond before turning to introduce Alex and Todd.

We shed our coats and muddy boots in the foyer and venture into the main living area. Todd has already started a fire in the large stone fireplace, and the flames are reflecting off the windows that wrap the living room and offer views of the nearby ski slopes. We all grab some pizza and a beer and sit down on the overstuffed furniture in front of the fire.

I look over at Todd. "I was telling Alex earlier today that you haven't heard from the police recently. I assume that's still the case?"

"Yep, not a peep," Todd replies while still chewing his pizza.

"Good news," I reply.

Todd nods. "As I said on the phone last week, I think that bodes well for you Mattie. In my humble opinion, if they haven't uncovered something at this point, I think it's pretty unlikely that they will. I mean, you have to figure that the Schuyler House investigation has run its course by now. Plus, I read an article somewhere that said very few art crimes are ever actually solved. I think it said that something like less than ten percent of pieces are ever recovered, and the prosecution rate is even lower than that."

"Wow, I hope you're right, but I am not letting my guard down just yet," I say as I take the last sip of my beer.

After we eat, Todd confirms that he has finalized all the arrangements to set up a college fund for Sarah's kids and for the donation to the environmental conservation fund in honor of Kat. I ask him if he's talked to Sara's ex-husband Jake about the college fund.

Todd nods again. "As you know, Jake and I were never very close, but I can tell the poor guy is really hurting. When they were married, he pushed Sarah to keep up her 'hobby' as a thief because he loved the money it brought in, and then he blew through it like a jackass. I realize he didn't even know about the Schuyler House until after it happened, but Jake is well aware that Sarah was struggling financially because of him, and he thinks her financial woes were what drove her to keep at it. Then she goes ahead and dies during a burglary. I think Jake feels like he's at least partly responsible for her death. He called me a few times right after Schuyler House. I think he was just looking for someone to talk to, and I'm the only person he can really talk to about the burglaries."

"Anyway, I called him again last week and told him about the college fund. He just broke down crying. He said he knew how worried Sarah was about saving for college and how much it would mean to the boys. He also asked how I knew about the fund since, as far as I know, he has no clue I've been in contact with you and Ellen. I just told him that I'd gotten a call from a lawyer in New York and that a trust had been set up for the boys…I tried to be as vague as I could."

We each have another beer, and Alex asks Todd and me what Kat and Sarah were like.

A smile crosses my face as I think of them. "Well, they both had the best damn sense of humor," I say, and see Todd smile as well.

"I remember the two of them poring over boring art research and giggling like school girls. Somehow, they found amusement in everything. Sarah always had on her lucky Red Sox hat, and Kat was always wrapped in multiple layers of clothing in an effort to stay warm."

"Kat was feisty as hell," Todd adds. "She never let anyone push her around, and I loved that about her. And she was so darn smart."

"Sarah came off as tough, but that's just because she was so matter-of-fact. She actually had a really soft side to her once you got to know her," I say.

"Those two were a bad pair. Always up to something," Todd says with a laugh.

I nod. "God, I remember this one time that Kat somehow decided it would be fun to go winter camping. I'm not sure how she convinced all four us to go, but she did. I think she told us it would be good team building." I smile as I think back to the trip. "We nearly froze to death, and Sarah was afraid to go outside the tent to pee because she was sure she was going to get attacked by a cougar. I tried to tell her that cougars were all but extinct in our area of the country, but she would have none of it."

"They sound wonderful," Alex says. "I'm sorry I never got to meet them."

Finally, Todd turns to Alex and me. "Well, I should probably head back home."

"It was really awesome to see you, Todd," I say as I stand to give him a hug good-bye.

"You too, Mattie," he says, and turns to Alex. "And it was great to meet you, Alex."

After Todd leaves, Alex and I play a few mean rounds of gin rummy in front of the fire before we both start to yawn and decide to call it a night. All that hiking wore us out.

CHAPTER THIRTY-SEVEN

Alex and I hit the road back to DC first thing Monday morning. I offer to drive for the first few hours so that Alex can catch up on some phone calls and emails. I know it's a big deal for her to be out of the office on a weekday during the peak season, but she doesn't say so. We pull into a rest stop just past New York City to get some gas and switch drivers.

As soon as we're back on the highway, Alex turns to me. "Okay, so we just pulled a couple million bucks out of a fucking tree. I can't wrap my head around it at all. It's totally insane. I am dying to know more about what you, Ellen, Kat, and Sarah did to generate that kind of dough. You've given me the short version of your, shall we say, 'tainted' past, but I want details."

At this point, I trust Alex with my whole heart and she deserves to know more about my past. "Hmm, well, gosh, I'm not sure where I should start," I mumble.

"How about starting by telling me how you guys decided where and what to rob?" she suggests.

"All right. Well, Sarah and Kat did most of the research, and they would usually propose places that they thought we should target. Usually, they would also recommend the actual pieces they thought we should go after. Their proposal always included a detailed explanation about their reasons for choosing a particular place and the specified pieces.

"Once Sarah and Kat made a proposal, the four of us would talk it over at length. If the group decided unanimously to move forward, we would move to stealth planning mode. A key element of the planning was establishing a timeline—feasibly, how long would it take us to prepare, and was there a time of year or a date that we thought would be best to carry out the burglary. Once we finished the initial planning, the next step was to 'case the joint'—in other words, one or two of us would spend a good deal of time 'on location' actually observing the next place we intended to rob."

Alex nods but keeps her eyes on the road, so I continue.

"Overall, I think we've pulled off nearly a dozen heists."

"Ooh, tell me about the boldest one," Alex says.

"Okay." I pause while I try to think of one of our most intriguing burglaries. "One of our first burglaries was from this office building in downtown Atlanta. We grabbed a couple of pretty valuable contemporary art pieces that hung on the walls of a very large and very prominent law firm. Honestly, I don't think the firm had any clue how valuable some of their art was. The firm's founders purchased most of the pieces back in the early 1960s.

"Anyway, Sarah and Ellen made an appointment—using fake names, of course—to meet with one of the associate lawyers at the firm just so that they could get inside the office and have a look around. They flew down to Atlanta, met with the lawyer and then spent a few days casing the office building from the outside. Not surprisingly, the building had pretty good security for people coming and going through the main entrance, but Sarah and Ellen noticed that there were some serious security lapses in the rear of the building. They observed that numerous office workers came down to the loading dock to smoke, and while they did so, they usually left the back door propped open. It didn't escape their attention that one of them was an overweight older woman whom they'd briefly encountered during their appointment at the law firm. She was a chain-smoker, and she came down to the loading dock almost every hour on the hour. She would always set her badge and pack of cigarettes on the bench next to her while she took long drags on her cigarette and scanned Facebook or whatever on her phone.

"The following day, Sarah and Ellen returned to the office building at the end of the workday. Sarah jumped up on the loading dock and was positioned on the bench when the chain-smoker came down for her last smoke of the day. Sarah pretended to puff on an e-cigarette while she took a glimpse at the woman's badge. The chain-smoker's name was Connie, and she was indeed an employee at the law firm. When Connie headed back inside, Sarah followed her. Connie took the freight elevator back upstairs and used her badge to get back inside the glass doors of the law firm. Sarah didn't try and follow Connie into the firm but hung around outside in the elevator lobby so that she could confirm the time at which the firm's receptionist left for the day." I pause and look over at Alex. "Am I boring you to death with too much detail?"

Alex briefly takes her eyes off the road to look over at me. "No, not at all. I am absolutely fascinated. Please go on."

"Okay, then. Well, anyway, Sarah's research indicated that more than five hundred people worked at the law firm's Atlanta office, and they were spread over three floors. As a result, we decided that it was highly unlikely that Connie knew everyone who worked at the firm. So, Kat and I flew to Savannah a few days later, rented a car and drove to Atlanta to meet Sarah and Ellen. We spent a few days finalizing our plan and buying supplies.

"When we were ready, we sent Sarah and Ellen back to the loading dock in time to once again catch Connie on her last smoke break of the day. Sarah perched herself on the bench to wait for Connie, and sure enough, she showed up right on time, propped open the door and sat next to Sarah on the bench.

"Ellen paced along the loading dock pretending to be on a personal call while ensuring that the loading dock door stayed propped open. As usual, Connie puffed away while staring at her phone. This made it easy for Sarah to swap Connie's badge for a fake one that we had made up the day before—it looked just like Connie's real badge, but obviously, wouldn't work to open any doors. When Connie finished smoking, Sarah got up too and rode the freight elevator back upstairs with her. Sarah made sure she got off the elevator first, and when she and Connie reached the glass doors of the law firm, Sarah swiped Connie's real badge and they walked in the office together. Connie soon left for the day and likely didn't realize until the next morning that her badge would no longer open any doors.

"Sarah just hid out in an empty office until the receptionist left for the day and then texted us to let us know that the coast was clear. Ellen stayed on the loading dock while Kat and I took the freight elevator upstairs. We assumed that many of the lawyers, especially the younger ones, would stay and work late into the night, so Kat and I were dressed to look like men and we were each wearing a jumpsuit with First Class Art Restorers stamped on the back.

"When we got upstairs, Sarah let us into the law office. Kat and I located the three pieces that we wanted and just lifted them off the wall, right under the noses of the lawyers that were still toiling away just down the hall."

"Wow!" Alex says when I finish. "You make it sound so easy."

"Well, we planned meticulously, so the heists *usually* went off without a hitch."

"Until Schuyler House?"

I nod.

"What did you do with the art after you stole it?" Alex asks next.

I tell her all about the arrangement that we had with Olivier, and then she asks me what our most lucrative burglary was.

"That's easy," I say. "It was the two pieces we stole from a billionaire's house in Texas."

"How the hell did you manage that?"

"Believe it or not, it was not as hard as you'd think," I say with a laugh. "The billionaire was a big donor for the Republican Party, and he regularly hosted these elaborate $5,000-a-plate fundraisers at his enormous house outside Houston. So, like in Atlanta, Sarah and Ellen went to Houston to do their usual reconnaissance except this time they had to pay $5,000 each to attend one of his dinners.

"Sarah was one of the most liberal people I know—she was a diehard Bernie Sanders fan—so it damn near killed her to pay money to help elect some right-wing wacko, but she did it, and according to Ellen, she did a damn good job of playing a Republican! Shit, she even wore pearls!"

Alex lets out a loud laugh and gestures for me to continue.

"Anyway, Sarah and Ellen had made some keen observations while they were at the fundraiser. They noted how the caterers worked and how the event was choreographed. All the fundraisers follow the same agenda: cocktails followed by a seated dinner before the crowd is summoned to the ballroom for dessert so that they can listen to remarks from the candidate for whom the fundraiser is being held. Our research indicated that the billionaire always used the same catering company, and they usually arrived in three vans—one with the staff and the other two full of food and liquor. Getting people liquored up was always key to these fundraisers!"

"Did Sarah and Ellen steal the art that night?" Alex asks.

"No, Kat and I attended another fundraiser at the billionaire's house a few months later, and that is when we stole the art. As luck would have it, both the pieces that we wanted hung in the dining room. After dinner, Kat and I hung behind in the dining room while the rest of the crowd was herded into the ballroom for dessert. The catering staff was scurrying around serving everyone dessert before the candidate's remarks, which left me and Kat a few minutes alone in the dining room before the caters came back in to finish clearing the dinner tables. That gave the time that we needed to slip two paintings off the wall and roll them each in a tablecloth.

"Once we had the pieces, we bolted through the kitchen and took off in one of the catering vans. We drove the van about two miles down the road where Ellen was waiting in a getaway car."

"Holy shit, you are kidding me!" Alex utters. "No one in the kitchen tried to stop you?"

"Nope. Some of the catering staff was in the kitchen when we ran out, but it all happened so fast and we were out of there before they had a chance to realize what was going on."

"It all sounds totally insane to me. Why did you guys take such crazy risks? I mean, what on earth made you do it?" Alex asks.

"I don't know what made us do it," I say seriously. "I mean, the money was nice, but none of us *really* needed it. Sarah has some financial problems, but, as Todd mentioned, they were more a symptom of the burglaries—her ex dug them into debt. As you can tell by the loot we just recovered, I never even spent most of share. I can only speak for myself, of course, but I guess it was the thrill that enticed me. That, and maybe the appeal of trying to solve a puzzle…how to find a small crack through which we could slither and grab the art."

"I'm sorry, I don't see the appeal." She laughs. "So, what are you going to do with all the money?"

"I don't know yet," I say honestly. "I need some time to think about it." I wish I could give her a better answer, but I don't have one, and she doesn't push the point.

We drive in silence for a little while before Alex asks, "So, did you ever try to find out what became of the pieces that you handed off to Olivier? I know you said that you don't know what he did with them, but you must have been a little curious about where they ended up."

"Believe it or not, no, I didn't. I completely threw myself into scripting the heists, but once the art was handed off, it was out of sight, out of mind for me, and I turned all my attention to the next heist in the pipeline. For me, it was all about the plotting and planning side of it. And, since we're on the topic, I never saw any news stories reporting the return of any of the pieces that we stole, and I don't know if any of them were ever recovered. I know that Sarah tried to find out what happened to the pieces we stole from the billionaire in Texas, but I don't think she was able to find out much about what ultimately happened to them."

* * *

It's late when we finally cross into the District, and Alex turns to me. "I'd love for you to stay at my place tonight, but it would make me nervous to have all that cash just lying around."

I smile back at her. "I understand. I'll buy one of those big metal safes tomorrow, I promise."

Alex pulls up in front of my apartment and double-parks her truck so she can help me haul the backpacks full of cash and my bag of clothes up to my apartment. Once the cash is safely inside my apartment, I pull Alex into my arms and give her a quick kiss on the lips. "Thanks again for going to Vermont with me."

"You're welcome, Mattie. It certainly was an adventure. I had fun!" She pauses, and I sense that she has more on her mind, but she reaches for the door. "I should probably go," she says reluctantly. "My truck is double-parked. See you at the office tomorrow? Oh, and don't forget, we're supposed to have dinner tomorrow night with Karen and Meg."

"Yep, I remember dinner. Looking forward to it. See you in the morning," I say before giving her one last kiss as she heads out the door. If Alex's friends have expressed surprise that she is dating a woman after being married to a man, she's never mentioned it to me. Like her, her friends are pretty laid-back, and my guess is that they just roll with the punches—if Alex is happy, who are they to question it?

After Alex leaves, I pick up the two backpacks and carry them over to the kitchen counter. I make sure the window shutters are closed and slowly unload the cash and pile it up on the kitchen island. When I'm done, I just stare at it.

It was true what I told Alex, I don't know what I am going to do with it. My financial future is far from certain at this point so, for now, I just want to hold on to the money so that I have some sort of a nest egg. Deep down inside, I hope with my whole heart that Alex and I have a future together, but I want to take things slowly and not put too much pressure on her. Maybe, someday, she and I can find something to do with the money together.

I finally snap out of my daydream and try to think of the best place to hide the money until I can buy a safe the next day. Putting it under the mattress seems a little too cliché and will probably be the first place a crook would look if they were to break in to my apartment. Finally, for lack of a better idea, I bury half of it under my dirty clothes in the hamper in the bathroom and jam the rest of it in my freezer.

CHAPTER THIRTY-EIGHT

I get up early the next day and head to the office. Unsurprisingly, Alex is already there. I poke my head into her office. "morning, early bird. Trying to catch up after I dragged you to Vermont for three days?"

Alex looks up at me and gives me a broad smile. "Good Morning. Yep, feeling a little behind, but as I said last night, I am *really* glad that I went along."

"Me too," I say softly before wandering over to my desk and flipping on my computer.

Sometime in the early afternoon, my grumbling stomach finally causes me to lift my head from my computer and take a break. I grab a veggie wrap from the food truck that is always parked outside the office and then take Uber up to Home Depot so I can buy a safe.

Home Depot has a larger selection of safes than I expected—they've got about fifty sizes, most of which claim to be fireproof, bulletproof, waterproof, you name it, and half of which appear to be for gun storage. I settle on one that is about three feet high and can be bolted to the floor. The thing weighs a ton, so I arrange for Home Depot to deliver it to my apartment between five and seven o'clock that evening. Alex and I are not scheduled to meet Karen and Meg for dinner until seven thirty, so the timing should work out well.

Alex is out at a worksite when I get back to the office, so I drop her a text to tell her that I have to run home after work but that I'll meet her at Nora's, the restaurant where we are meeting Karen and Meg.

The delivery guys show up with my safe at 5:03 p.m., and while they unpack it, I ramble on about how excited I am to have a place to store the letters my grandfather wrote home during WWII. It's my very lame attempt to allay any suspicions that they might have about what I plan to store in the safe. I ask them to place the safe in my bedroom closet, and they tell me that I have to hire a handyman to actually bolt the thing to the floor. I make a mental note to ask my elderly neighbor for the name of the handyman she uses. After the delivery guys leave, I gather up the cash from my hamper and my freezer and load it all in the safe.

* * *

I get to Nora's a little before seven thirty. I'm the first one there, so I grab a seat at the bar and order a glass of white wine. Alex, Karen, and Meg all appear a few minutes later, and we follow the hostess to our table.

After we order, Karen turns to Alex. "Soooo, how was your little getaway to Vermont?" she asks with a wicked grin.

"It was…great!" Alex gives me a knowing smile.

"You two are such little lovebirds," Karen crows. "So, what did you do…and you can spare me the details on the sex you had! I haven't touched a man since Doug and I broke up!"

Alex and I both laugh. "We visited a few of my friends," I respond cautiously.

"And we did a little hiking," Alex adds innocently as she grabs my hand under the table and squeezes it.

Three Months Later

Eventually, I start working at Hemlock full-time. I still primarily work on the finances, but I also start to get involved with more aspects of the business. I even enroll in a few landscape design and horticultural classes at George Washington University to expand my knowledge of plants and trees and other landscape-y things.

One night after work, Alex and I decide to have dinner at Coppi's, the cozy, wood-fired pizza place where we had our first unofficial date. The restaurant is unusually quiet, but it's a summer weeknight so I guess that's to be expected. Congress is out of session and the rest of DC has likely fled to the beach. The hostess leads us to one of the few booths, and we decide to share a large Margherita pizza.

Alex reaches for my hands after we order. "So, I've been thinking." She looks at me tenderly. "What would you think about moving in with me?"

I look back at her and feel an almost overwhelming rush of emotion. It takes me a minute to find my voice. "Really?"

"Yes, really. I want to share my life with you, Mattie."

"Nothing would make me happier," I say finally. My eyes are moist, and I dab them with my napkin.

Alex and I promptly order a bottle of champagne. It doesn't really go with pizza, but we don't care. We've got something wonderful to celebrate.

* * *

Alex agrees reluctantly to let me bring my safe full of cash to her house when I move in. Every week or so, I take a small amount of cash out of the safe and deposit it into the Hatshepsut checking account. I only deposit a little bit at a time because I'm very conscious of the Bank Secrecy Act which requires banks to report any *cash* transaction of ten thousand dollars or more to the IRS. Basically, if you deposit more than ten thousand dollars in cash at a bank (and the key here is cash), the bank will ask you for identification because they have to file some form with the IRS to report the deposit. The law was established to catch people trying to launder money (which I guess technically includes me). And the IRS isn't totally stupid, they make banks report deposits that even look fishy—a person purposely trying to skirt the law by making multiple deposits of $9,999 or even two $5,000 deposits made in one day, for example.

So, because of this law, it's going to take me a very, very long time to move all the money out of the safe and into the Hatshepsut account for safer keeping. But I plan to keep at it until the safe is empty.

Regardless, I plan to save most of the money, although I am not totally averse to spending some of it here and there. In fact, I just booked Alex and me on a two-week vacation with some fancy outdoor adventure company. According to their colorful brochure, we'll hike, bike, and kayak through a bunch of National Parks but stay in nice hotels at night. I really want to take Alex on a bike trip through Tuscany, but I guess that will have to wait for another day. For now, I need to stay stateside.

Bella Books, Inc.

Women. Books. Even Better Together.

P.O. Box 10543
Tallahassee, FL 32302

Phone: 800-729-4992
www.bellabooks.com